AT THE SEAMS

Pamela Gwyn Kripke

(PUBLISHED BY OPEN BOOKS)

Published by Open Books

Excerpts from this book were originally published in
Embark, The West Trade Review and *Meet Me at 19th*.

Interior Design by Siva Ram Maganti

Cover image © by Danielle Balderas
shutterstock.com/g/Danielle+Balderas

For Mom and Dad

PART ONE
1968

ONE

As a child, my mother fell asleep listening to the adults at the end of the hall. It was the 1940s, when relatives visited each other in the evenings and sat up and talked. They spoke about the baby sometimes, the baby boy who had arrived a few years earlier than she did, with blue eyes and his mother's skin, pearly and light.

He slept in the hospital nursery, as all infants did then. The nurses brought him to my grandmother at feeding time, delivered on a cart with the other newborns, in a row, swaddled up. Weighing nearly ten pounds, he was positioned on the end, where there would have been more room.

After a few days, he didn't come. Instead, the doctors asked my grandfather to give blood. They didn't tell him why, even while the tubing ran from his arm. Soon afterward, they said that the baby was dead. Without warning, without reason. *Your baby is dead. Your just-born, healthy baby boy is dead.* My grandparents begged, wailed, pleaded, but no one said anything. Not ever.

From her bedroom down the hall, curled up in evening's grainy haze, my mother heard the rise and fall of voices, the careful words, the jittery words. The theories. She heard what her father came to believe but could not prove, that the baby had rolled off the end of the cart to the floor. That he rolled off the cart, and no one was there to catch him.

During the course of a routine conversation when I was eight, so routine that I cannot place its day or time or location, my mother told me the story. She said she didn't know for certain what had happened, when it had happened, if the infant even had a name. But the voices sailed through the hall and into her consciousness. They said that the baby was robust and pink, but then he was dead.

Maybe there was no room in the middle of the cart for a baby of ten pounds, or maybe the nurses thought he'd push one of the smaller ones off the edge with his strong big-baby arms. There were no sides to the cart, no wall to roll into on a fast trip, a swervy trip, a careless trip. It was like a cart in a library, I imagined, or something from a restaurant kitchen. Maybe they used it to distribute meatloaf and peas when they didn't pile babies on it, when they didn't press them together, arm to arm like hotdogs in cellophane. Like cigars in a box.

Anyway, my mother told me she didn't get out of her bed and ask the people about her brother; she didn't even say that he was her brother. He was *the baby*. The dead baby. Hush. Don't say anything. Don't repeat this. Don't ask a soul or say that you know. It will only upset Grandma Lilly. Again. We don't want to upset her again.

She gave me no lead-up to the story, no situation that needed explaining, no rationale for the tale to be told. We could have been talking about vegetable soup, or dancing class. We could have been baking a cake and cutting it into shapes and turning it into an elephant, following the directions in the blue booklet, with the drawings of the lions and bears. We could have been saying or doing nothing at all.

It's entirely possible that my mother simply said, "So, you know what happened? Grandma Lilly had a baby and the baby died, and Papa Sam chased a nurse down the street, right down the street to ask her why. But she ran away, she ran away so fast that he never caught up."

It's entirely possible that my mother said that, that she looked at me with her deep brown eyes and in a swoop flung open a curtain, snapped up a shade, revealed a world that I didn't know existed or could exist so close to my family. So close to me.

The number of U.S. ground troops in Vietnam peaked in 1968. My dad turned on the television every night after dinner, and I watched the war footage. Soldiers, in black and white. Trenches, smoke. Helmets. I remember the helmets, and the guns, and the reporters shouting over the noise. My parents let me see it, even though I was only in second grade. Maybe because I was in second grade. Not a toddler, not a teenager, but old enough, important enough. No sheltering here.

Bad things could happen, I knew, from watching the screen, from hearing about wounds my surgeon dad sewed up at night while we slept. But they happened elsewhere, in places where there were jungles and enemies, or where Presidents had motorcades, or where black pastors stood on balconies, defenseless. They didn't happen on Rolling Way.

The 1960s were all around us—the suburban barbecues, the go-go boots, the air-raid drills. We sat under the curved staircase on the lower floor of Ward Elementary, a hundred kids cross-legged on the terrazzo tile, the yellow fallout shelter sign on the wall above us. We weren't told exactly what it was for, but we knew the whirling black triangles didn't mean a fire or a bad storm. They didn't signify something we had experienced. So, we sat under the staircase, protecting ourselves from something different, something from far away, something that could reach us in our classrooms but not under the stairs. Watch out. Duck and cover.

Still, despite the mixed signals and vague explanations, I felt certain that nothing would fall on our heads at Ward Elementary—not a bomb from the Soviet Union, not a rocket ship from Mars, not the roof from a hurricane. There was unrest in some places, but my neighborhood, my house, my world were all safe.

———

It was in town that Papa Sam recognized the nurse, in the weeks or months after the baby died. Was he there alone? Was he with my grandmother? Did he turn and say, "Lilly, stay here. Don't move." Did he take her with him by the hand, her charm bracelet marking the pace? Or did she say, "Sam, don't run. Leave it alone, let it be."

The story my mother heard claims that he got close enough to ask a question, to project it down the Belle Harbor sidewalk, but that it dropped to the pavement, unanswered. Seeing him coming toward her, weaving through pedestrians maybe, picking up speed maybe, feeling desperate maybe, the nurse fled, turned a corner, lost him. That alone was confirmation, the voices said at the end of the hall in my mother's house. That alone proved something had gone awry. The assertions whooshed across my mother's room and into her ears. A compassionate nurse, a person who knew a man had endured an excruciating loss, would embrace him, would see him coming and hold out her arms. A nurse who was not aware of something to conceal would not have run. Even a nurse who was aware of something to conceal would not have run, unless she'd panicked.

Nothing about her actions on the street gave solace to my grandfather. Nothing about her response led him to think that his infant had died a natural death.

I found a baby bunny in our backyard. At the end of the lawn, our property rose up into The Hill, an expansive, tiered incline. We didn't hike up it every time we were in the yard, or plan ahead to make the journey. The urge would come without warning, finding us between whacks of the badminton birdie or pendulums on the swing. Exploration, conquest, the pull of the wild. My older brother Ben and I felt the lure of nature, of flora and fauna, even if that lure was confined within the property lines behind our split-level in New Rochelle, New York. Our suburban expeditions up the hill, scaling pachysandra, stone, and soil, were monumental treks to us, feats of daring and strength. I knew to put on socks, as Mom had planted low-lying shrubs with prickers.

The hill was terraced, the levels marked off horizontally with walls of gray rock about a foot high. We began at one end of the yard, near the fence that separated our lawn from that of our neighbors, the Brants. Methodical kids, we traversed the width of the hill, pivoted at the end, and proceeded to a higher altitude, weaving our way up like yarn in a loom. We rarely hopped levels, unless Jimmy

Brant accompanied us skyward. Jimmy Brant pushed the limits. He would later become a music industry executive.

The bunny was by itself near the bottom of the hill, no family in sight. I picked her up and held her against my stomach. She was small, no more than six inches long, brown and gray and soft. Her ears stood straight up, and her eyes were sweet and bright, ringed in white fur. She didn't try to get away.

I carried her across the yard to the kitchen door and called to my parents. In the garage, my mom found a cardboard box, in which I placed grass and twigs and leaves, lettuce, carrots, water in a dish. Ben and I had wanted a dog, but my parents rejected the responsibility of that, thinking we were too young to take care of a warm-blooded being and not wanting the chore themselves. So, we had goldfish and turtles, animals in bowls that we could not caress, or talk to face to face, or walk on a string—animals in bowls that required a sprinkling of food and not much else. Knowing this, defying this, I would put my hand into the water anyway, attempting to make contact, to create a bond, to love my pet and be loved back.

The bunny was a cuddly mammal, similar to a dog, and it entered my life willingly and—crazily, in retrospect—without parental prohibition. City folk who had not grown up with cats or puppies in their homes, my mother and father had little rapport with the kingdom.

The next day, we went to the pet store and bought a cage for my wild animal. It had an aqua-colored metal base and chrome slats. I put the bunny through the door, along with her water and vegetables. She explored her home, and I sat on the garage floor and watched as my new friend adjusted. I felt that I had saved her.

When my mother told me about the baby who died, I was confused, but mainly frightened. I had become accustomed to her unconventional nature, her breaking of rules, but this was different. I felt thrown, the way she probably had when the voices sailed through the air into her room decades earlier.

But that had been accidental; my mother chose to reveal the information to me. I couldn't understand why she told me not only about the fact of the death but also its violent details. Why did I need to know? Or why, more likely, did she need to let out the story, to hear it said in her own hushed voice, like a secret, and then warn me to keep it one—to keep my knowledge from my grandparents, as she had done. Why load me up at eight years old with the scary death of a person who could have been an uncle, who could have looked like my mom, or me, who could have painted and sewed as we did, who could have crossed his arms that way, our way, when he walked? Did I need to know about him for some reason, a reason that she didn't understand herself? Was she trying to make sense of the death, after so many years, by saying it out loud?

She had probably been the same age as I was now when she found out. Did she want me to have the identical experience? The identical horrible experience? My mother had friends, colleagues, many other grown people with whom she could have shared the story. But she told it to me. Why me?

On my bunny's third day, I took her out of her cage and carried her around our property. She didn't seem to want to jump away, but still, I didn't put her on the grass. In my mind, she was mine. I had made her mine, determined that she would stay with me because I wanted her to. I didn't put her down because that wouldn't have been safe—safe for me, for my emotions, which had become entwined in possessing the rabbit, in dictating her whereabouts, her activities, her relationships, her very life.

We had freedoms as children. We rode our bikes until it got dark, wherever we wanted to go, except for the big streets. No Quaker Ridge Road. No Victory Boulevard. We went outside to play and returned hours later, having visited our neighbors' houses, gone to the school playground, run through sprinklers. I suppose that a lot of what we did at that age, in those times, was dictated by feel, but we also made decisions. We weighed pros and cons, we considered what we knew our parents would advise, for or against. We did not intend to be mischievous, nor did we view our freedom as an opportunity to be disobedient or reckless. Maybe my parents knew this and trusted that we'd manage the choices we encountered during our adventures. They exerted pressure when it came to school, but in our leisure life they believed we should make our own fun. So, we scaled the hill, hid under the Brants' willow tree, caught wild rabbits. *Caught wild rabbits.*

On the fourth morning, I went into the garage to check on my bunny, to feed her fresh lettuce and fill up her water bowl. Still in my pajamas, I pressed open the electric door and walked to her cage, the morning light spreading across the floor. She had been awake when I arrived on the previous days, roused by the rumbling of the door or, more likely, an innate internal clock. She had looked at me and sniffed through the bars. This day, she lay on her side. I dropped to my knees on the cement. Her body was still. I called to her, afraid of what she looked like. Horrified. Guilty. Panicked.

I screamed for my parents and ran inside to find them. My father had left for the hospital, and my mom was in the kitchen making breakfast. She followed me to the garage, picked up the cage and took it away, disappearing around the side of the house. I stood by myself, sobbing, shaking. When she came back, she said something about keeping a wild animal captive, how it wasn't a good idea. Then she went back to the kitchen.

I was an obedient child. I would have said, *Okay, I'll let the bunny go back to the hill.* I would have been disappointed, but I would have understood that it was where she came from and where she needed to be, that somewhere on the hill her mother was waiting. I would have understood that and wanted to return her. I would have scoured the hill for her mother, brown and gray and just a bit bigger, a bit fatter. I would have swept aside the thorny bushes, peered between layers of rock. I would have made it my mission to reunite the wild animals, and I would have done it, or done something close. But no one told me it wasn't a good idea to capture a wild rabbit, and no one told me he was sorry when she died.

My mother put the cage on the shelf over the hood of her car. It sat on the edge, among beach chairs and winter boots. Every time I went into the garage, I saw the chrome bars flash as the electric door rose, pummeling me in the stomach, making me wince and look away. One day, after school, I dragged a cooler over to the shelf, stood on top of it holding a broom, and jabbed the cage until it was out of view.

TWO

MY MOTHER TOOK OFF for school each morning in the Chevy Monza, a blur of fabric and scent. Cristal, by Chanel. She carried a carpet bag with leather handles, cut from an Oriental rug. In the evenings, she lifted the flap and spilled papers onto the floor of my parents' bedroom. Dittos, they were called then. Worksheets made on a machine that cranked out copies from purple carbon paper, by hand. If you held the paper by your nose, you could smell the fluid. Intoxicating, it was, like rubber cement and strawberries. A bottom drawer in our kitchen was filled with unused sheets, for games of tic tac toe, hangman or shopping lists. After college, she followed her father's lead and started out as a buyer in the apparel business, fulfilling orders in New York for stores that didn't have a representative in town. It was a fashionable job for a fashionable young woman. But after she had my brother and me, my father convinced her to become a teacher. He wanted her to have an enduring skill of her own.

Mom learned on the job and developed a style; hers grew more from instinct and personality than pedagogy. She liked the little ones, the sweet little ones, with the raincoats they couldn't zip, the astonishment that flushed their faces when they shook heavy cream into butter. She liked the singing in a circle, the growing of plants, the learning of script. A couple of times a year, my school wouldn't be in session when hers was, so she'd scoop me up from home at lunchtime and take me back to her class. The halls of Roosevelt School were quiet and the classrooms orderly, teachers in front of the boards, children obedient in their seats. Pass by them and take a look, one by one, and the scene would be identical. But at the end of the corridor, waiting for Mrs. Nichols, a bustle of small children rolled on the floor, jumped in the air, zigged and zagged like bees from a hive. As we got close, the kids grabbed her by the hips and held on, asking where she was, why she was late, and whether I had anything to do with it, whoever I was.

"Is that your daughter?" they'd ask, and then fall over, stunned, offended, even. Sometimes, they called her Mom. I'd sit at her desk while she taught, look in the drawers (a mess), sort through her magic markers (the caps mismatched). There was typically a naughty student pulled up alongside, playing with the paperclips or stapler or *World's Best Teacher* letter holder, whatever was within reach. He, and it was invariably a he, would try to get my attention, by muttering about my mother or talking to me directly.

"She wears that orange coat," or "You don't look like her," or "Maybe you do."

Mom gave me tasks to do to keep me busy...water the plants on the sill, stack papers or rearrange supplies in the cabinets that ran low against the walls. Mostly, I organized her desk drawers and cleaned off the surface, but the order confused her natural state and left her itchy.

On our way out of the building those days, Mom whisked me by the hand into each room, including the Principal's office, before everyone went home. A Principal's office is a bad place, even if he isn't yours and he's being nice. I said yes to whatever he asked. One by one, the other teachers hugged and squeezed me, exclaimed something encouraging and inspiring, and tilted their heads the way teachers do when a star student does what they expect her to do. I felt like a special kid with expectations to fulfill. And that was okay. I was nothing if not dutiful.

It was clear to me that I had an unconventional mother. She did not succumb to rules, and her disregard for them was brisk. At the town pool, she concealed her jug of homemade iced tea behind her beach chair and lured us to take illicit swigs on the grass rather than in the designated picnic area. To avoid a crowded store dressing room, she had me try on clothing (over and under what I was already wearing, thank god) in the middle of the aisle. "No one is watching, Kate," she'd tell me, when everyone was. Once, when she didn't like something that my father said, she flung a melamine plate across the kitchen. A Frisbee. It would happen again. Frozen rolls, a bag of peas.

Teaching redirected her spontaneous spirit, a bit, anyway, and it gave her voice and friendship. She and her colleagues played doubles tennis on Tuesday nights. They took belly-dancing classes in our basement, wearing genie pants and belts that jingled coins. Sitar music streamed from the air conditioning vents into my bedroom while I did my homework. The women shared joys and losses, taking care of each other in school and out.

Her work showed me who my mother was, who she was beyond the walls of our eclectically-styled house a half hour north of Manhattan. When she went on strike for better wages and benefits, we drove by in the Bonneville to lend moral support. I spotted her on the sidewalk, marching with her fellow teachers, holding a sign she painted in our garage the day before. Dad stretched his hand out the window and made a "V" with his fingers, and I did the same. He honked the horn, and we cheered. We cheered like loons. At age eight, I got a sense of justice, and what you do when you don't have it. And I felt, from the back seat of Dad's sedan, the mettle of my mom, underneath the Sassoon haircut and geranium pink lips.

Not all mothers had jobs outside of the home in the 1960s, and I loved that my mom did, and not only because she let me unwrap the Christmas presents that her students gave her or brought home sticks of chalk for our box ball courts. I loved that she was committed. I loved that she did so much with her days. I loved that despite it all, I felt that my brother and I were always first.

THREE

THE WEEKEND AFTER MY mother told me about the baby, we went to my grandparents' house. The route took us past a massive water tower shaped like a southern biscuit. *Belle Harbor* was painted in green script along the side that faced the parkway.

As a young child, I thought that Grandma Lilly and Papa Sam lived inside of the tank. Of course, now I knew they occupied the blue half of a navy and white two-family on Neptune Avenue, a block from the beach. I knew there was a short driveway, a terrace and three steps that led to the front door, and I knew that these parts of the house, and all of the others, were not wet or flooded or floating. I also realized that my father did not drive our 1968 Pontiac Bonneville up the spiral steps wrapping the water tower that proclaimed the town's name, or have us get out of the car and climb the stairs to the top. We did not dive, seated in the vehicle or uncontained in the air, into the vat high above the Grand Central Parkway and swim our way into my grandparents' living room, where roast chicken waited on pedestaled trays. Yet, beginning when I was old enough to remember and for some years afterward, I thought that we had. Somehow, once inside the tank, I believed it was possible for us to carry on as we did and remain dry in the process.

As much as I was an imaginative if not delusional child, Lilly and Samuel Goldman inspired such fantastical notions in my developing brain. Lilly and Samuel Goldman were magical.

Papa Sam kept one unsmoked cigar tucked into the top of his sock. When he walked, the cellophane crinkled against the leg of his trousers, and it sounded as if he in fact had water-tower water in his shoes or had forgotten to take a tag off from somewhere. After dinner, he went out to the porch, lit the cigar and sucked in his cheeks, closing his eyes halfway. He blew stunningly round, delicately lined rings of smoke that rode the beach air like bangle bracelets, keeping their shape high above Neptune Avenue, out toward the Atlantic.

After dinner, Papa Sam and I sat on the metal glider while the sun went down. Everyone else was inside the house. He took off his glasses and rubbed his neck.

He worked hard during the week, running the dress company that he had launched twenty years earlier, a few years after the end of World War Two. He named it Lill-Dor Fashions Inc., for Lilly and his mom, Dorothy, and set up shop at 152 West 36th Street, an elegant eight-story building in the beating heart of Manhattan's garment district.

He blew a trail of rings over the railing and said that the seagulls caught them in their beaks and carried them across the town, placing them on the heads of sleeping children.

"On all of them?" I asked.

"The unusual ones," he said. "The ones like you."

Then, he slipped a coin from behind my ear and twirled it in his fingers, his eyes widening.

I grabbed his hand and then the other, peeling them open, finding nothing. "Show me how."

He took another quarter from his pocket and sat closer to me on the glider. I held my hand out, and he placed the coin inside my palm, curling my fingers into position one by one. "Now, watch closely…"

I mimicked his movements, fumbling at first.

"Make it look like a bird." His hand became a wing.

My grandfather embraced the make-believe, and there was a spirit about him that was unlike that of anyone I had encountered. He had an aura of possibility, a love for the dream that drew me to him, that made me feel we were on some quest together, even though we never said what that pursuit actually was.

I wanted to ask him about the baby, despite my mother's instructions. If he could explain it to me, I would feel better, less afraid. I wouldn't have to startle, anywhere, anytime, jolted by thuds on linoleum, screeches from white-capped nurses, mounds of men flailing on the floor. He would tell me that it never happened, that my mother was just imaginative like me, that she used to dream up tales and act them out in the living room, that she mixed up what was real and what wasn't. Papa Sam would straighten it out. He would make it disappear like the coin in his hand. I watched him flutter his fingers and swivel his wrists, mesmerized himself by the trick or the movement or the moment.

"Here, try again." He folded the quarter into my palm. "You're a natural."

The porch door opened and slapped shut.

"I know how to do that," said Ben.

Papa Sam put down my hand and turned to him. "You do, do you? All right, Benny, let's see."

The evening became suddenly practical. I watched my brother perform the trick, pretty well, I must say. Papa Sam snuffed out the cigar and laid it on the edge of an ashtray. I thought about the unusual sleeping children, haloes on their heads.

———

That night, Ben and I were going to sleep in the den on fold-out couches. I said that I was tired and went into the room early, before my brother. I didn't know what I was looking for, but I opened the drawers of my grandfather's desk and flipped through papers and composition notebooks and folders tied with string. I pulled open cabinets and found Frank Sinatra records and old bottles of liquor wearing tuxedo vests to soak up the drips. In a closet, I saw a stack of photo albums, each one four inches thick. I dragged two off the shelf and sat on the floor. My heart sped. Maybe there was a picture tucked away. Or a tiny hospital bracelet, sliced for removal from a tiny wrist, pressed flat.

I turned the pages, seeing my grandparents blow out candles and drink daiquiris, pose in front of Radio City, eat corn on the cob.

They smiled for the camera, sparkly, full of life. I opened another book and saw my mom, about my age at the time, on a sidewalk with her grandmother, Beatrice, who used to come on the bus in a long black dress and dance when she stepped onto the pavement. She came most days, but the joy didn't wear off.

The den door creaked, and I quickly gathered the heavy books and pushed them back onto the shelf.

"You have to see this one," Grandma Lilly said, placing two extra blankets on a chair. She stood on her toes and reached an ivory album. "It's Evie, the first time we took her to the beach. Look how beautiful."

My mother was in a carriage, a sailor hat square on her head. Grandma Lilly traced her fingers over the stroller, around its big white wheels.

"She looks like Ben did," I said.

Grandma Lilly put a finger on my mother's cheek. "She does... she looks just like him."

In the morning, Papa Sam scrambled eggs, lifting them a foot out of the bowl like stretched taffy. Ben and I perched on ice cream parlor chairs and drank real orange juice, not the frozen kind my mother squeezed from its can and mixed with the tap. Grandma Lilly entered the yellow kitchen in a floral caftan and pom-pommed slippers, her salon hairdo peeking from under a colossal bow. She turned her index and middle fingers into four Rockette dancing legs, pressing their pink-painted tips on the table and raising them into passés and kicks. While she sang, Papa Sam presented her with a gold-edged cup and saucer, into which he poured her coffee, tipped from the waist, dish towel over his arm. She dropped tiny white pebbles of saccharine into the cup and dripped milk from a spoon. "Explosions," she called them. She let me drip the milk if I asked.

It was a beautiful day, every day, Papa Sam always said. No matter what, he made it seem so. They could have lived inside a water tower, without question.

———————

Grandma Lilly had a favorite color, which, for a sixty-seven-year-old woman, could have seemed peculiar or trifling, but she didn't care. She told people that she lived in the top apartment and that it was blue, which was fortuitous, as she loved the shade, particularly the deep tones, the aquamarines.

It was a strangely warm weekend for late May, so we went to the beach. Grandma Lilly took us by the hand to meet her neighbors, bending under their umbrellas and calling to them sideways.

"Yoo-hoo, Emmie, yoo-hoo," she said, pulling me to her. "Look who's here to see me. It's Kate and Ben. Look at them, my, my."

Each morning, and sometimes during the day, Grandma Lilly swiped her chest and arms and backs of her knees with a powder puff, emerging from the bathroom in a jasmine cloud. Under Emmie's umbrella, pressed against my grandmother's bosom, I sneezed from the talc.

Before she allowed us back inside the house, we rinsed off under a shower in the yard.

"Go between your toes," she said. "Every tiny one."

The stall had a white wooden door that clapped, and leaves and vines made their way through the slats. I was accustomed to baths, inside of a house, in a room decorated with flocked velvet wallpaper. On the stone floor of my grandparents' outdoor shower, I threw my eyes up to the sky, incredulous.

On Sunday, my father timed our departure so we wouldn't get caught in traffic. He had to be at the hospital at seven the next day, and Mom, also, had an early start in the classroom. Sunday nights were for preparing. They were serious. My hair was wet from the outside shower when we got into the car, and my skin was still hot from the sun. The beach does that to you, mixes up your senses, distorts time. Grandma Lilly gave us a shopping bag filled with turkey sandwiches, pickles and peaches. Combined with the linger of suntan lotion and salt air, the aroma was nothing that could be duplicated anywhere else at any other time.

Grandma Lilly and Papa Sam stood on the sidewalk and waved as we pulled away from the curb. Just a couple of inches taller, my grandfather rocked on his toes, one hand overhead, the other around Lilly's shoulder. I swiveled around and waved back out the rear window until I couldn't see them anymore. If we got caught at the light on the corner, I could watch them turn and go up the steps. That Sunday, I saw Papa Sam hug Grandma Lilly at the front door, and they stayed like that, her head on his chest, until the light turned green.

Everything they said or did now, every look, every motion, had new meaning. Was an extra embrace at the door meant to ease a sadness? Was a funny remark meant to distract? A complimentary one intended to compensate? Had their entire existence, their cores, their personas, been transformed by tragedy? Did I not know who my grandparents truly were?

In the car, I remained awake long enough to consume a full turkey sandwich with Russian dressing and a half a pickle and not long enough to determine if we drove the Bonneville from the depths of the water tank, blasted through the surface and sped down the spiral steps to the road.

FOUR

SAM SPOTTED LILLY ON a New York City subway platform in the late 1920s. Mom says it must have been her legs. Or eyes. Or the combination of the two. Delicate ankles and green orbs, like bottle glass.

Sam knew beauty, or I should say, he knew form, balance, precision. A patternmaker for a dress manufacturer in the garment district, then, he could turn sheets of oaktag into curvaceous arms, hips and busts, without even measuring. He learned the craft on the job, having to quit City College mid-stream to help support his family. The second child and oldest son, Sam rode the train from the Bronx to Manhattan each day, and he took a sketchbook with him for the commute. Years later, after he launched Lill-Dor and he and Grandma Lilly visited us in New Rochelle, he drew pictures of dresses and suits and jackets, legs and arms and necks, rapid fire. Add a belt, I'd tell him, mesmerized. Now buttons. A cape.

It's possible, given his zeal for fashion, that Sam was attracted to the cut of the coat that Lilly was wearing, or the pleat of the skirt or choice of length, nap, collar or sheen. It is certainly plausible that he would have noticed a certain plaid or spin of a hem from where he stood down the subway platform, and that he was drawn to the garment and not to the wearer, no matter her ankles or orbs, as unromantic as that would have been. Or, it might have been that so taken with her clothes, he was consequently taken with her, because she had decided to wrap herself up with such intriguing choices that day. While technically gifted, my grandfather was above all else artistic, and he loved the fantasy of the art. My hunch is that to him, the woman imbued the creation that enveloped her with something of herself, and the handiwork did the same in return. For Sam, I believe, the edges of the relationship were fuzzy, like a lush bouclé.

In the 1890s, Sam's father Bernard arrived on New York's Lower East Side from Russia, where he had learned to sew. He went to work in one of the neighborhood's garment factories, first making shoes and later, dresses, and ultimately owning his own company. Lilly's parents, too, were Russian immigrants who would come to own a dress manufacturing business, and as Bernard Goldman did, Abraham Rosinsky would pass along the family trade to his children. Fashion was embedded in my grandparents' DNA.

When they met on the New York City train platform, it was a tumultuous time for the country and for Lilly. People had endured a World War, the first deadly brush with polio, the 1918 influenza pandemic. The stock market crash of 1929 was imminent, as was Abraham's death. Lilly's two brothers had relocated to Virginia to work as jobbers, buying clothing surpluses and selling them to stores across the South. Her sister had gotten married and moved out, leaving Lilly at home with Beatrice on Crown Street. Lilly worked as a saleswoman in a millinery shop and took care of her mom, who could speak English but not read it or write. My grandmother used to teach her how to spell. When Lilly and Sam married in October of 1931, the bride wore pale blue, still observing the traditional year of mourning for her father.

While at home one afternoon, Lilly saw a reflection of a man in her bathroom mirror. He was behind her, climbing into the house through a window. She screamed at him, and he turned and ran out, the way he came in. People lost everything in the stock market crash, and men who normally wouldn't break into another person's home found themselves slithering up brick facades and prying open panes of glass. Lilly didn't know if the man wanted money from the box tucked deep in the chest of drawers or food from the kitchen, both of which she would have given to him had he rung the bell and asked or stood on the street and asked.

Sam had held onto his patternmaking job, and though Lilly had lost hers in the hat shop, they were careful savers and had enough money to make it through and even a little left over to share. But after the man climbed through the window, Lilly was afraid to sleep and eat and bathe on the ground level, separated from the unpredictable course of the day by mere stucco and stone. So, they moved to the top floor of the two-flat on Neptune Avenue, where the layer of people below provided security for Lilly, the way a poor swimmer finds comfort in the sight of a flotation device, even if clothed and on land. From the picture window and, when Sam wasn't blowing the rings, the porch, she watched the street, high above its speed and strangers. An owl in a tree. They never again lived on the first floor.

Sometime between the break-in and 1935, when my mother was born, they had the baby. I imagine Grandma Lilly wearing maternity dresses that Papa Sam designed for her at the factory. She is thrilled and apprehensive, worried about knowing what to do with an infant, how to feed him, change him, soothe him. She holds her belly with her arms, cradling it from underneath while she stands and sits, while she walks. Rubbing it when it moves. And on The Day, the thrilling and scary day, she calls across the blue house to Sam to come help her, to guide her down the staircase and out the front door and into the Oldsmobile parked by the curb.

Every couple of years, Sam brought home a new car. Fascinated with gadgets and machinery, he traded in the old one and returned with a more modern model. Knowing that Lilly would be angry with his purchase, despite it being his only indulgence, Sam kept the cars a secret until the last possible moment. When they drove up to our house in New Rochelle, he did the same.

"Look outside, Katie," he'd say from the foyer, motioning his head toward the driveway.

I knew what was out there. The surprise was the color, and the name that Papa Sam had made up for it..."Pretty Lady Green" or "I Love Lilly Blue."

In my mind, I see my grandmother sprawled in a diagonal across the bench seat, her hands stretched wide over her midsection. With each intake of air, they float up and off her mound of a stomach and down again. When they arrive at the hospital, she pushes herself up on her elbows but collapses with a thud into Sam's rib cage.

"Help me, I can't do it. I'm too big," she says, wobbling side to side like a canoe. "I can't believe how big."

"Here we go, Lill. I'm going to raise up your back," he says. "Now hang on."

Sam runs around the outside of the car to open her door, and a nurse meets him with a wheelchair.

"Well, you look ready to have a baby, don't you?" she says to Lilly. "How are you feeling?"

"Dreadful. I think I'm going to have it right here."

"Don't worry, dear, you'll be just fine. Come along, Mr. Goldman. And leave your car key with the nice young man in green."

Lilly moans in the chair, bent, her breasts flattened and splayed on top of her belly. Inside, a young girl takes them to a room and recognizes Lilly immediately. She tells her the gift shop never looked so beautiful before Lilly came to volunteer. She had rearranged the displays, adding tulle and rick-rack that Sam brought home from the factory.

Within the hour, Lilly is wheeled off, and Sam goes to a room where the fathers wait. On a table is a radio with a blond wood finish, curved top and black dials. He pushes the button and smiles. Duke Ellington. "Satin Doll." Sam steps back from the window and with his right hand just below his ribs, his left one outstretched, falls into a Lindy on the checkerboard tile. Sam's version is a fluid pouring of rhythm and glide, a visionary approach, really, to the classic dance. He tosses in triplets when no one is looking and extends his leg out, in front and even back, while his partner spins.

Mid-stride, the doctor enters. Sam takes off his cap and smooths his hair straight back, adjusts his jacket and his belt and even his socks.

The doctor gathers Sam's shoulders in his long arm. "Everything is perfect," he says. "Your Lilly is waking up right now and the baby, well, the baby looks like you. Let's hope he's as good a dancer."

Sam spots Lilly way at the end of the recovery room in the last bed and speeds down the center aisle. Lilly sees him and raises both arms up over her head, then flops them down, groggy. Sam buries his head in her neck and starts to cry. She smells like the brown soap in the upside-down bottles in the hospital bathrooms.

"Did you see him, Sammy? Did you see him? They said he's a handsome boy."

Right then, a nurse appears cradling a white blanket. A sleeping face with mile-long lashes pokes out.

Sam takes his son from the nurse and introduces himself. "Hello, there," he whispers, his voice breaking. "I'm your daddy. I'm your daddy Sam. And this pretty lady is your mother."

"Oh, Sam, look at him," she says, her eyes tearing. Lilly takes her child and pulls him to her chest, rocking forward and back.

Sam sits next to her on the bed, a threesome, and they sway gently into the night.

FIVE

WE LIVED AROUND THE corner from school, so my brother and I didn't have to take the bus. Sometimes, I waited for him at the end of the day, since his class ended later than mine, but mostly, I walked home by myself. I liked the time alone. I counted the mailbox flags—how many up, how many down. I analyzed the house windows—bay or double-hung. I collected rocks and dandelions, fed leftovers from my lunchbox to beetles and ants. If Gail Rimpelman skipped up behind me, I was okay with it but was happier when she peeled off at Stanhope Road.

After my mother told me about the baby, I was scared to walk home by myself. I was scared to arrive home first and be alone with her, fearing what she might say next. My parents were my entire world, and the notion that I was avoiding one of them distorted everything.

So, I began waiting every day for my brother. I told him that I had something to do after school for Mrs. Colson, but I was really camouflaging myself behind the bus kids until he came out. The truth was, in my seat in class, the news penetrated my body. The activity and the assignments couldn't distract me. In fact, the attention to earthquakes and powers of ten, to concepts that were irrelevant to babies and hospitals and mothers who said too much, found no place to settle in my brain. I wanted to know every detail about the incident, but I was also petrified to know. The place above my ribs got tight and quivered like a snare drum. My pigtails stuck to the sweat on my neck. Breathing hurt. Mrs. Colson called on me, and I didn't know what she was talking about or whether her voice was coming from her mouth or the ceiling or the bowels of the building's basement.

Each day after lunch, we wrote in black-and-white composition books, and this was the only task that I could complete. It was the only time the pencil didn't slip in my fingers or my heart didn't reverberate in my skull. I was scared to death when my mother told me about the baby, and I had no idea what to do.

"What were you doing for Mrs. Colson?" Ben asked, coming out the school door.

"Helping her clean the erasers."

Ben nodded. "Fun job."

I wanted to ask him if he knew about the baby. Mom said to keep it quiet, but maybe the dictate didn't include my brother. How could it not include my brother? My parents raised us as twins, after all, since we were only fifteen months apart. Mom put us in dueling toggle-button coats, and wherever my brother went, I accompanied him. No activity was deemed too advanced, too proprietary, too male. When he and Jimmy Brant threw footballs on the back lawn, I played, too, grabbing the laces, sending spirals into the grass. Later, when Ben formed a sixth-grade band with the lanky Spector brothers, my mother instructed him to find a role for me. It was determined that I would stand in front of the boys and dance, go-go style. I know now that he must have been wholly annoyed—with my mere presence, let alone the prominent placement of my person—but he didn't let on. I was his biggest fan.

I watched him walk down the sidewalk, up the hill by the Freed-lands' house and around the curve. I watched him talk about hitting the erasers on the brick and the way the art teacher looked like a walrus and how he got to spit into a tube during a science experiment. He had no idea, moving naturally through his nine-year-old world, that we had an uncle, a dead baby uncle, a dead baby uncle who had pulverized my expectations and understanding of all things. *All things.* He had no idea whatsoever. It was completely on me.

We had three houses left on the sidewalk side before we crossed the street, pressed the garage button, ducked under as the door rose and entered our home. At the first house, the Ressovutos', I told myself I'd say something by the time we got to the hedges on the far side of the driveway. We passed the lawn, one of the nicest on Rolling Way, and the stone path on which Johnny Ressovuto stood on the tips of his sneakers like a prima ballerina. I stared at the hedges as they came toward me, emerald green boxes that made their intentions clear to the Thompsons beyond, particularly their Pekingese, Paul.

"Mom told me..." I heard the words emerge from my lips.

Ben looked my way. His little-man haircut shivered in the breeze.

"She told me the other day that..."

"What?"

He could repeat it, and no one was supposed to know. I couldn't disobey.

"...that we might go to that park, with the sprinklers, maybe."

Ben said something, but I didn't hear what. We passed the Thompsons' house—Paul barked at us from the bay window—and then the modern one after it, where the teenagers lived. I went straight to my room and closed my door halfway. We were not a family that shut them completely.

Angie Mae Fowler was our housekeeper, a sound and durable woman who lived with us in New Rochelle during the week and returned by train to Brooklyn on weekends. She was reserved and sturdy, about fifty. She sewed her own dresses and sang at church. Angie wasn't effusive, but she was a rock, reliable and kind. She cared for us, as we did for her.

Angie dusted and vacuumed, managed the laundry, and handled all other chores while my mom went about unleashing the imaginations of New Rochelle's six-year-olds. Most important, though, she was present in the afternoons, and she prepared dinner. My mother did not like the kitchen.

When I asked Angie to sit with us for dinner, she said that she had work to do. So, on weekday evenings, as she prepared, I went downstairs to help her. Afterward, I cleared the plates and some-times made up things to do in the cabinets or the sink when she sat down at the table. I learned her daily schedule and hurried to make my bed and straighten up my room before she came upstairs. No toothpaste hit the bathroom sink.

My mother's heels clicked across the tile in the den and up the first set of steps to the kitchen.

"Hi Angie, kids home?"

Angie began dinner early, and the smell of browning chicken swirled up the second set of stairs and into my room.

"And what did you put in that pan? Mmm, I don't know how you do it."

"Nothing special, just plain old chicken," I heard her say.

"Plain old, right. You've got secrets, Angie Mae."

Angie laughed. "And you might check on Kate," she said, after a beat.

I stiffened and got closer to the door to listen.

"What do you mean?"

"Well," Angie said, pausing. "I'd check on her."

Mom headed up the second bank of stairs and into my room, where I had snatched a math workbook out of my school bag and tak-en it to my desk. I pretended to work on a problem and slid around in my chair when she entered. If I appeared busy, she wouldn't stay long. My parents left us alone when we did our work, firm believers in the benefits of struggle.

"How was your day, sweetie?" She sat on my bed, the straps from her carpet bag and purse slipping off her shoulders.

I avoided her gaze. "We had gym, so good."

She held a stack of mail and her shoes. The barrette that clipped her hair to the side was crooked and useless, nearly poking her eye. Her lipstick had worn off.

"That's right, Tuesday."

Mom looked at me and tilted her head. "So, do you want a snack before ballet? I bought the cheese that you like, with the cows on the wrappers."

"Maybe," I said, turning back around and picking up my pencil. "I'm going to finish this now."

She got up, walked over to my desk and felt my forehead. I gripped the pencil with a fist.

"Hm," she said and headed for the door. The back of her shirt was untucked and wrinkled. Her feet tapped like Grandma Lilly's. After she left, I jumped up and pressed my face into the mirror to see if I looked sick.

I had a doll in a pink floral dress. She had sprays of blond hair and huge brown eyes. Under the dress, she had a second head, this one sleeping. The floral dress became pajamas on the other side. In the morning, I used to take Nighttime Baby from her cradle, wake her up and flip over her clothes, turning her into Daytime Baby. I thought the doll was ingenious. From my desk chair, I looked at her, sitting upright against my orange wall, and I shuddered. Living Baby, Dead Baby. I picked her up and threw her into the back of my closet.

———————

That day at school, I had written a letter to my bunny in the black-and-white composition notebook. I tore it out when Mrs. Colson wasn't looking and brought it home. From the inside pocket of my briefcase, I pulled out the paper, which I had folded four times.

Dear Maisy,

I am so sorry that I caught you and put you in a cage. I won't ever do it again, I promise, even though I will never forget being your best friend. I love you and I miss you.

Love,
Kate Nichols.

I got cellophane from the kitchen and wrapped up the note, taping all of the edges. On the front, I wrote Maisy's name in pink marker and drew a heart. When it was ready, I went outside to the spot where I found her and tucked the paper deep inside the wall, in between the layers of rock, until I couldn't see it anymore.

I sat next to it on the stone and looked up at the back of our house, counting seven standard windows, a double for the kitchen and a sliding door to the den. The Brants had additional windows in their garage, with planters, and I perceived their configuration to be somehow better, more extravagant, more current. I surprised myself, realizing that I hadn't quantified our rear window formation in so many years of looking at it.

Behind the master bedroom window, my mother was changing out of her school clothes into pull-on pants and sneakers. Ben was in his room, playing his sparkly silver drum set, sending paradiddles into the air like Morse code. Angie was chopping cucumbers for a salad. Three distinct compartments, like televisions dialed to their own scenes, fulfilling some individual purpose but held together in a box. From the window in my room, just over the desk, my eyelet curtain flapped against the screen, a magnet to the wind. I could be in there now, doing my vocabulary homework, putting on my leotard, but I am out here, outside, making amends, looking in.

Six

AN HOUR LATER, I unraveled my pigtails and made a high ponytail.

Angie waited with me by the front door. "No bun today?"

"It's okay."

"Come, you've got a minute."

I sat on the foyer bench while Angie took out the bobby pins from my ballet bag. She tightened the elastic and twisted my hair, wrapping it around itself and inserting the pins, making my head feel solid and balanced.

"Now you're good," she said, cupping my chin in her hand.

I heard my mother on the stairs and gathered up my bag and sweater.

"Thank you, Angie," I said, hugging her waist. I walked out the door to the driveway. My bun didn't jiggle no matter how I shook it.

———

Miss Kellerman's School of Ballet was five minutes away by car, located in a sprawling old Victorian with a wrap-around porch. The main studio, where the older girls had class, occupied the former living room, a massive space with a high ceiling and windows on three sides. The older girls got to wear pink tights, with seams up the back. We wore all black, like little spiders, and would until we turned ten. Our studio was adjacent and less grand, a smaller parlor or sitting room of some kind. Ballet, and the training of ballerinas, is predicated on hierarchy, and everything about Miss Kellerman's enterprise on North Avenue oozed of ranking. The piano player or the records. The dressing room or the hallway. Front row or back.

First at the barre. Second. Last. Quickly, we learned that this structure was to be embraced rather than contested. We were riveted
when an older girl came in to demonstrate. We pointed our toes
until our arches ached, extended our legs until they trembled. We
knew to be patient. Skill would come.

My mother pulled up in front of the mansion to drop me off. She
was a stranger in the car, like someone else's parent. Her revelation
changed how she appeared to me, now shrunken and curved rather
than regal, gaudy rather than chic. Dizzy, I grabbed the door handle
and stiffened in the seat.

"Why did you tell me what you told me?" I said, finally.

She turned around and held the headrest. "What do you mean?"

"The baby. I don't want to know about it," I yelled, opening the
car door. "It ruined everything."

She thought for a moment. "My mother's baby? It happened. I
don't know what else to say."

I slammed the door and ran down the path to the house. Inside,
I went straight to the bathroom to gather myself. A bowl of soaps
shaped like toe shoes sat on the sink. I splashed cold water into
my mouth and on my face and neck and arms and pressed it into
my skin. Class would be starting, and I couldn't be late. I splashed
again and dried myself with a paper towel, before squeezing in
among my classmates on the hallway floor, trading my sneakers for
slippers, tucking the drawstring and flattening the elastic on the
top of my foot.

I leaned back, breathing hard, and waited to hear the reverence
through the wall behind me, the curtsy at the end of class. There
would be muffled applause, and then the door would open and the
younger girls would file out past Miss Kellerman. Each one would
thank her. Then, it would be our turn.

My classmates came from all over town and other places, too,
and I felt connected to them. We were somehow different once inside Miss Kellerman's house, stripped down and revealed, engaged
in just one pure pursuit. One perfect pursuit, in which only pliés
and turns and leaps mattered and all else remained at bay. Instantly,

the scent of lambskin and hairspray suspended our lengthened and centered torsos, our turned-out feet, our stretched necks, and we felt like fairies and princesses but mostly like little girls who were doing something extraordinary and becoming so in the process.

We took our places at the barre and stood in first position. Miss Linda, who would start the class, lowered the needle onto the record. My knees bent in plié and my chin lifted, and for an hour and fifteen minutes, I tried to forget that I would dream that night, as I had every night, of tiny boy babies tumbling from the sky like hollering hail and landing at my slippered feet.

After class, my father was waiting for me in the vestibule of Miss Kellerman's studio. He had come to pick me up instead of Mom, a rarity given his hospital schedule.

"You feel like taking a detour?" he asked before turning the ignition. "Maybe getting something cold and delicious?"

"The Checkerboard?"

"I don't get to pick you up every day, and I could use some lemon-lime. What about you?"

The Checkerboard was what we called the Italian Ices place near the high school. It had no sign, so we named it for its black and white floor. A man dove into the freezer to scoop the ices, pressing them into pleated white paper cups, piling them with a spade like teepees. We didn't go to The Checkerboard often; it was for occasions.

"Strawberry! No, wait, root beer!"

"That a girl," he said. "Off we go."

We sat on the bench outside the shop, talking about dodgeball and spelling words and the gall bladder he took out earlier that day. I knew about veins and arteries and nerves and tendons. He taught me a mnemonic device for remembering the bones of the wrist and another one for the parts of a cell. It was strange to me that other kids didn't know these things.

"Mom won't like that we've eaten dessert before dinner," Dad said when we were about finished, handing me another napkin.

I looked at his face, his sweet hazel eyes and dimpled chin. "I yelled at her before."

"I know."

"What's a transfusion?"

Dad stopped eating his lemon-lime. His expression didn't budge. "She said that Papa Sam gave one."

Dad wiped his hands and lips and folded the napkin into a square. He answered slowly. "It's a way people can help someone who doesn't feel well, like medicine. That's what the word means."

I felt the tears shoot through my face and burst out. Geysers. I fell into his chest. "She told me about Grandma Lilly's baby. Why did she have to?"

He wrapped his arms around me. "I'm not sure."

"Did it happen? Did he fall on the floor?"

I felt him tense slightly. He looked straight at me, blinking once. He didn't know that she had said so much. "We don't really know. I hope it didn't happen, but it's terrifying to think about it." He put his hands square on my shoulders. "It's normal if you're afraid."

"Can you make her not tell me again?"

"She didn't mean to frighten you."

"I can't get it out of my head."

He smiled to encourage me. "Mind over matter. This may not have been as bad as you are imagining. Tell yourself it's sad, and feel sad, but nothing more because we don't know any more."

I flattened the pleated paper cup and squeezed the remaining drops of Italian Ice into my mouth, trying to figure out what my father was instructing me to do. I could have certain feelings but not others. I could be sad but not scared. And I could do this if I just told myself to do it, like one of Papa Sam's magic tricks. But where would the other feelings go? The real ones, would they evaporate or migrate somewhere else and hibernate? Could I choose to visit them, to get just close enough, to poke a stick at them like a hive of bees? Dad was implying that by deciding to minimize the feelings, they would disappear. As much as I wanted to believe that, I doubted it could happen, to me, anyway.

We drove home past Miss Kellerman's School of Dance, its windows lit up at dusk. I could see the older girls crossing the floor practicing piqué turns, heads whipping around, legs in passé. In my seat, I curved one arm in front of me, extended one to the side, and began the count. On two, I pulled the stretched arm in with the force needed to spin. And again. And again, seeing myself travel, but too dizzy to know where to go.

SEVEN

WHEN MY MOTHER WAS a sophomore in college, she asked her parents which of two suitors she should choose, having slid seamlessly into the social whirl that 1950s Boston afforded to a pretty girl with New York pedigree. She rode in parades atop convertibles. She tailgated. She dined and danced, sartorially prepared for any eventuality, having been raised in a dressmaker's home. A separate trunk was necessary for transporting just the crinolines to Charlesgate Hall, her freshman dormitory on Beacon Street, as a streamlined version of the turn-of-the-century petticoat was enjoying a resurgence when my mother matriculated, underpinning a skirt or dress with lift and kick. Boys called on the phone, made dates, waited downstairs in the lobby for her to descend, cat-eyed and coiffed, pointy-pumped, dabbed at the wrists in Arpège.

For all of her sheltering—Grandma Lilly used to ride in the school station wagon with her and the other first graders—my mother emerged as hardly the awkward only child. Rather a fun-loving socializer, she made fast friends, carried herself confidently and kept up her grades. Independence suited her.

One of the interested boys, Daniel, stood to inherit Rhode Island's most profitable textile company and drove a turquoise Cadillac, outfitted with boat tags. His family kept a small yacht on Narragansett Bay, and Daniel often left campus to host parties on board. Once, he picked my mom up for a date wearing a ripped white T-shirt, à la Marlon Brando. Another time, he leaned against a pillar in the dormitory lobby holding a pink cigarette, to match the stripes in his shirt.

It's said that in the forest, the antidote for poison ivy comes from a plant that typically grows close to it. Jewelweed, it's called. Its sap is medicinal. Nature seems to do this, to put competitors in proximity. To help? To challenge? To be cruel?

Richard S. Nichols was jewelweed sap in the forest of collegiate courtship. The boy who was to be my father was a poorly dressed and underfunded medical student who needed a date to the annual school dance and couldn't procure one himself, having befriended only books, fellow male students and cadavers in his two years at graduate school. A mutual friend introduced him to my mom, an undergraduate six years younger, and she accepted his invitation. The evening of the event, the Boston rains did what they do, pouring down sheets, walloping gusts, rendering hats and coats and umbrellas laughable. Not a night for peau de soie pumps. Richard borrowed his brother-in-law Roger's well-worn Hudson and after the party, he drove my mother back to Charlesgate. He didn't call her again until one year later, to the day. He said that she needed to have that time to mature. Then, after he felt that she had, in fact, done that, he laid out his entire schedule for the following six months, including exams, hospital rotations, nights on and off. A man of science.

At the appropriate moment, when my father was due to graduate and leave Boston, my grandparents arrived on campus to interview both boys. Grandma Lilly believed that Daniel would be entirely more fun but that Richard was solid and earnest and that was better, if you were going to be a husband, which was the leap people made when you went on a date in 1956.

Lilly peered down at him from the hotel window as he walked into the front door. "We'll get him some new suits," she said. "Shoes, too."

———————

My mother accepted the fraternity pin. It still hangs from a charm bracelet, resurrected decades later when chunky baubles were all the rage.

Dad did his surgical training at Cornell in Manhattan, and my mom transferred to New York University after the first semester of her junior year. Dad once again borrowed the Hudson from Roger and drove my mom and her crinolines south, this time in a New England snowstorm. The Hudson's windshield wipers were no match for the onslaught and en route, they gave out and blew off—right off!—left, right, gone. Swept up in wild winds. Catapulted onto Storrow Drive.

A few weeks before her graduation, my parents married at the Essex House on Central Park South. I have a dinner menu from the wedding, a diminutive blush pink booklet tied with a tassel. Art nouveau lettering. Filet mignon with béarnaise. My dad's mother, Nana Sofie, wore a rose lace-topped gown from Papa Sam's line, off the rack. Lilly's dress, of course, was tailored just for her. Following the ceremony, my mother skipped the graduation festivities and the newlyweds honeymooned in Haiti. My father had just one week off in June, so they scheduled accordingly.

In 1958, women were routinely given anesthesia during childbirth. For the most part, they fell asleep, gave birth and woke up. My mother fell asleep, gave birth and woke up, at which point she tried to rip out her IV, fly out of her bed and bite the medical professionals taking care of her. One out of eighty-nine million women had a perverse reaction to the anesthetic; Eva Nichols was the one.

A week later, having regained her composure, she and my brother left New York Hospital for home and began the mother-son dance, the singular tango of lead and follow, follow and lead. At twenty-three, my mom had limited experience with infants. With my father at the hospital most days and many nights, she was on her own much of the time. She'd wrap up my brother and walk over to the medical center dining room for dinner, so Dad could see Ben awake. My grandparents helped, as surgical residents earned only seventeen dollars per week at the time, and my mom made neighborhood friends, other new mothers who walked the strollers together and shared advice.

Six months later, she was pregnant again with me. When she

arrived at the hospital, the doctors knew to avoid the sedative.

By school age, we expected that Dad would be home for dinner, despite how busy he was. He hurried, and we waited. Sometimes, an emergency kept him at the hospital, but for the most part, we all ate together. Often, he'd be called away afterward to tend to some burst organ or gunshot wound, which he told us about the next day, elucidating the critical lesson. *Get to a hospital for sharp pain in the lower right quadrant. Stay out of bad neighborhoods.* For a time, there was a rash of stabbings. *Choose friends wisely.* Dad learned to eat efficiently, and we made good use of his presence. He quizzed us on our homework, made sure everyone was being nice to us at school. If a utensil fell to the floor, we were to leave it there, until after dinner. O-R rules. Dad's own fork and knife became surgical tools in his hands; elbows out, focus sharp, slices clean.

Our house in New Rochelle was the first my father purchased, an achievement for a child of the Depression. It had a dogwood tree out front and a crab apple on the side. For my bedroom, I chose tangerine orange paint for three of the walls, and Mom selected paper for the fourth—pen-and-ink drawings of two French can-can girls, each four feet tall, wearing feathers and buttoned boots. I named them Fifi and Gigi, and it's quite possible—okay, quite certain—that I spoke with them from below before falling asleep at night. More than a few times, Ben showed up in the doorway to see what he was missing. It didn't take long for my father to peek his head in, too.

"She's talking to the wallpaper," said Ben.

"And what is wrong with that?" said Dad.

Lying under Fifi and Gigi the night after we went to The Checkerboard, I heard my parents arguing down the hall. I heard whispers and clenched lips, high-pitched bursts, stern declarations.

"I did not," my mother said.

"Never again."

"She'll be fine."

"So destructive."

"I didn't mean to," Mom said. "Don't yell at me." "Please, stop."

Their words sailed the hallway and whirled around my ceiling, piercing evening's grainy haze, lingering as similar adult talk had in my mother's house a generation earlier.

"What have I done?" I asked the drawings on my wall. What have I done?

EIGHT

WITH A PARING KNIFE, my father peeled orange and apple skins into single spirals of uniform width and depth, the fruits left naked and unscathed on a plate. I closed the ribbons back up into spheres, and it appeared that they hadn't been touched. Wizardry.

My mother would saw the fruit into indiscriminate wedges, leaving behind pools of liquid and half-chewed pulp.

If a matchmaker had been dispatched to the Goldman household, I wonder if she would have paired my mother with my father. It would have been one of those cases in which the arranger of the proposed union would tout the shared world view, the compatible values about what's really important in life. *What's really important in life.* She would minimize the opposing demeanors, the reserved versus the care-free, the preference for libraries instead of beaches, the early for the late. She would urge the Goldmans to think philosophically, not practically. She would marvel at the intermingling of so many fine characteristics within the same walls. She would entice them with the potential, convince them to disregard the habits and personalities and quirks and focus instead on the wisdom of the plan. And likely, the children whom they would create.

In theory, my parents had differences that could fill in each other's deficiencies, that could make them, together, a commanding whole. My dad's sensitivity could have defrayed my mom's empathy gap. My mom's frivolity could have helped my dad become more spontaneous. I wondered how they landed mid-stream.

———

I winced when I heard my parents quarreling that night, wanting to both muffle the conflict under my pillow and discern every word. They presented a dilemma, a weighing of fears. A dead baby on a hospital floor was a scary sight to have flying around in my psyche, but I was analytical enough and stoic enough to know that neither I nor anybody else I knew was in jeopardy. A tumble onto tile would not happen to me, or Ben, or even the newborn the Biddlemans just had down the street. What had happened was that my panic about it led to trouble between my parents. If I hadn't flopped like a weakling at The Checkerboard, my father wouldn't have confronted my mother, and everything would be as it was beforehand. Peaceful, harmonious, normal.

I had caused havoc, grave havoc between two people who loved each other and needed to keep loving each other, for everyone's sake. The notion that they might not was scarier to me than the infant's death, no matter how violent and disturbing and secretive it was. Stuart Surrey's parents yelled at each other at a Little League game, and a month later, Mr. Surrey lived somewhere else. Stuart and his sister Alice ran to the gate at the end of the field the second they spotted him, barreling across other people's picnic blankets and grabbing him as if he had just returned from Vietnam. He'd bring chips and grapes in supermarket bags. Mrs. Surrey had the cooler. The Surreys were instantly changed, no one doing what they normally would have. I would have died if my father lived somewhere else and brought supermarket bags of chips and grapes to a baseball game, if I missed him so much that I stepped on other people's ham sandwiches and containers of cole slaw.

I was responsible for the discord between my parents and feared that it could alter their course, and ours, in devastating ways. So, I needed to fix the situation I had created, and there was just one way to do this. I would buck up and ignore how the baby's death made me feel. I would determine not to be traumatized or unsettled or confused, following the pattern established two generations earlier. I would decide that my mother's revelation, though inappropriate and inciting, would not saddle me with moral predicaments that I couldn't manage. If I didn't, the consequences would be dire, if they weren't already: What if I had caused my parents to hate each other?

The plan was clear. If my imperfection had spurred this disastrous result, the remedy would simply be the reverse. I would have to be flawless. I would have to do exactly what was expected of me, even if it meant squashing my inclinations, my curiosity and my opinions. I would give up part of myself to keep our family together.

For the next little while, I tried to carry out the plan, earning accolades wherever they were given—school, ballet, the dentist. I was first seat in band, first to the finish line in the fifty-yard dash. I won spelling bees, essay contests and camp beauty titles. I even had friends, despite my rarified status. At home, of course, where I fulfilled all expectations and ceased any investigation of or emotional investment in my family's questionable history, my achievements were celebrated. Ben and I were busy kids, not allowed to be bored, but we also had a rich life finding our own way, swinging on swings, digging up earthworms, riding bikes. We got along and didn't rebel. Mom and Dad couldn't have had it easier, or seemed happier. The arguing subsided. I had saved them, and above everything else, this was my most glorious accomplishment.

NINE

AT FIRST, MY MOTHER sewed by hand, fixing what a typical family needed fixing in her spare time. She stood us in front of the full-length mirror, dropped to her knees and pinned up whatever drooped too low—skirts, dresses, pant legs. We took off the garments carefully and laid them in a stack on the ironing board, work orders. At night, after a day of teaching, she pressed them with steam, sat on the couch and sewed. My father had turned on the news or a police drama. The Man from U.N.C.L.E. The Red Sox. If something ripped, or a button popped off, we added it to the pile. Dad contributed socks, many socks.

Overwhelmed, Mom stashed her needles and bought a machine.

The motor unleashed her talent, revved up her technical skill and powers of invention. She dispatched the hems and repairs with speed, pulled by her genetic urge to create from scratch. Soon, we were spending Saturday afternoons in the fabric shop, flipping through four hundred-page pattern catalogs strewn on a massive table. I'd point to an illustration, and Mom assessed its viability, taking into account the opinions of similarly crafty women who shared the books. We started with skirts. Dirndl skirts, gored skirts, A-line. When we found one we liked, the clerk yanked open a huge file drawer and walked her fingers over thousands of white envelopes, locating the corresponding number and pulling out the packet. We took it to the bolts and searched, knowing that if we didn't fall in love, we had Papa Sam's factory scraps in the back closet.

At home, Mom unfolded the tissue paper pattern and spread it out on the floor. I gripped her scissors and slid the bottom blade underneath, lining it up and pressing down. Mom guided my hand around the shapes; soon, cutting them became my task. Though not a patternmaker like Papa Sam, my mother knew how to scale up or down, or alter a line. But she held firm to the original plan, trusting the model and adjusting it only to suit an aberrant dimension or creative impulse. She folded the fabric and smoothed it out, crouching over it on her shins, positioning the pattern and pinning it in place. Then, steady sounds of slicing rang up from the floorboards, evenly paced, firm.

The process was a ritual, from which we'd rise up, ready for thread, ready for the whole to bloom from the parts. At the machine, Mom was a pilot, commanding the controls, speeding up on the straight-aways, slowing on the turns. I stood to her side like an O-R nurse, catching the pins as she removed them, sweeping shards of cloth into the bin. Without warning, she set up a seam under the presser foot and stood from the chair. Nervous, I slid in and stretched my leg to reach the pedal. Go slowly, don't worry. I eased my toes down, eyes fixed on the needle, and fed the fabric through. Mom nudged it straight if I veered off course.

I wore the skirts to school, and also the dresses and tops and pants that came later, and I felt on those days shored up, encased in the pride that comes from making something yourself, from making something yourself with someone who loves you. No one knew that my mom sewed what I was wearing, that I helped cut the pattern and thread the elastic at the waist, that we had deconstructed my dad's shirt into a dress and trimmed it with ribbon and braid, that our ideas and mistakes and successes were embedded in the fibers on my waist and hips and legs. No one asked about my clothes, and I didn't volunteer. Making them was something that we did together, just the two of us. My mother didn't read books to me before bed. She didn't have long conversations. When we went to a museum, Dad taught us about the bison or the early settlers and Mom complained we'd hit traffic on the ride home. Our mutual creativity is what connected us, and I protected the bond, deriving a private strength from the experience, the knowledge that we did it ourselves and would do it again.

For my cousin's wedding, we selected a Dotted Swiss in deep navy and white. From the pattern drawer at the fabric shop, we found a sleeveless dress with an Empire waist and shirred skirt, a classic little girl silhouette. But the wedding was going to be at night, in a fancy ballroom. Mom hesitated at the cutting table; the clerk waited, scissors open.

It's got to be long, my mother realized, lighting up. And full. "Add a yard of the semi-sheer cotton, please, and two of the lining."

The bolts somersaulted, and the cloth rippled after them like a speedboat's wake.

I hadn't ever been to a wedding or worn a gown. Our New Rochelle den became a workroom those weeks before the affair. I wasn't going to be in the ceremony; the dress would not be on full view. Still, my mom devoted extreme attention to its creation. Sewing was the place where my unscripted, unrestrained mother became a perfectionist.

Dad stepped over the scraps to his favorite chair, newspaper in hand. "You two could have a cottage industry."

By that time in my apprenticeship, I could envision the finished garment from the illustrations on the pattern envelope, even with my mother's decorative enhancements. Not much was left alone. If a ruffle could be added, it was. If a waist needed a bow or banding, it got the treatment. The adaptations for the wedding frock, the simple addition of length and volume, would transform a stand-ard-issue school dress into something atmospheric.

We began the process, laying the fabric on the floor, pinning the pattern, cutting. The dress quickly became complicated, though, needing lining throughout. No raw edges allowed. None of the dresses or skirts that my mom had sewn for me until then had re-quired such fanfare or had that much physical weight. She could whip those up in an afternoon. The Dotted Swiss wedding gown would assume archetypal status in my blossoming wardrobe. In any eight-year-old's wardrobe, really.

Papa Sam was called in for reconnaissance.

The dart is the lifeblood of dressmaking. Waist darts, radiating darts, bust, neck, shoulder and underarm darts...these small folds, or narrow triangular tucks, give human contour to flat fabric. They are transformative and determining, elevating bolts of cotton, crepe, wool, and silk to sculpture. Yielding flair, elegance, spunk, they provide three-dimensional space for the female body, letting it move, breathe, flourish.

In the workroom, the patternmaker drapes, pinning sheets of muslin to a dress form and maneuvering them, creating the darts, and gathers and pleats, to fit, connecting the sections with seams, adding details. There are collars—flat or rolled, pointed, notched or shawl. Peter Pan, Johnny, Sailor or Military Band. And sleeves— from plain fitted to bell, bishop, melon, three-quartered. Puff, with a darted cap, a gathered cap. There are necklines to think about, and bodices and skirt slopes, and waists. Natural, blouson, cinched.

When the parts manifest a garment, when they merge into a comprehensive, glorious whole, it is peeled off the form like a membrane, laid out, and deconstructed into a paper pattern, from which one dress or a factory-full is cut and sewn. Its creator is both engineer and artist, technician and designer. An aesthetic wizard who also understands geometry, measurements and materials, who knows which shapes will translate across dimensions, which numbers must be calculated and abided, which fabrics can do what.

My grandfather's shears were more than a foot long. He lived with a tape measure hanging from his neck.

At home, my teenage mom was a junior designer, creating ideas in her head and seeing them appear in her closet a week later. For a high school dance, she designed a strapless, sleeveless dress that had a separate collar and cuffs, tailored as if cut from a man's shirt.

Thinking that her arms would look best utterly bare, she shaved them with a razor, unaware that they'd grow back, in thickets. Any garment that she and Grandma Lilly bought in a store was reconfigured, so they shopped the discount racks for clothes that held promise, knowing that Papa Sam could take them apart, perform surgery, and stitch them back together, improved. Often, the entire silhouette would be altered and accessories added where there had been none. Buttons here, a pocket there.

Decades later, when Ben and I were in elementary school, Papa Sam brought us boxes of fabric remnants, sequins and beads. And he brought us industrial-size spools of thread, wound in criss-crosses on cardboard tubes. We had every shade for every color—blues in tones from sky to cerulean, greens from chartreuse to deep forest.

———

My grandparents came early on a Saturday and spent the day, eager to help with the dress for the wedding. Grandma Lilly assumed observation and support duties from the marigold couch. She was an accomplished watcher, of pirouettes across the living room, drum riffs on the snare, skits. Hopscotch, running races. In Louis XIV chairs, cushy sofas, picnic benches, she sat the same way...back and head tall, legs together at the knees, feet close and straight ahead. Her hands clapped or danced or waved, rings and bracelets providing musical accompaniment and smiles, encouragement. She sang along when appropriate.

Our workroom/den was a mid-century fete of color and pop. Underneath the marigold couch was a pink and orange shag rug and beneath that, black terrazzo tile, speckled in white. Grandma Lilly turned sideways to observe the dressmaking. She had opinions, all of which would begin with "Sam."

"Sam, make the neckline rounder."

"Sam, show me the back."

"Sam, that's it."

I brought a pad of paper, coloring books and crayons over to the sofa while he oversaw the production of the lining. "It's like making two dresses, Evie. First, match up the seams at the neck and around the arms."

"Now pin?"

"Extra pins, then you'll clip and press. It's looking good, sweetie."

I prepared a page of paper for a huge game of Dots. "Pick a color."

Grandma Lilly chose turquoise. "That's going to be some dress."

Across the room, Papa Sam taught my mother how to coax the lining, to lure it to fit. He talked her through the zipper placement, fending off the frustration when the layers of fabric buckled or edges veered. The ultimate teacher, he didn't take over. He sat next to her on the floor, at the ironing board, at the machine. She was a willing student, and she was talented, with capable hands and an innate feel for how the fabric worked, what it could become. She seemed like a kid to me, asking her dad to fix a mistake, becoming antsy when he wouldn't. "You'll never learn if you don't try yourself, Evie."

We took turns connecting the dots and quickly, the board filled up with hatch marks, waiting to be finished off into boxes and claimed with our respective initials. Grandma Lilly had taught me how to play the game, and she was an aggressive competitor, inscribing her completed squares with luscious loopy L's and sailing her crayon overhead in a flourish.

"Where are your K's?" she teased me. "I don't see enough K's."

She counted the boxes, gold charms clinking on her wrist, and I wondered whether at that precise moment, that playful carefree moment, she was thinking about her baby. Was every brain cell devoted to the hunt for dots, or were some neurons engaged elsewhere, in the maternity ward, at the nursery window? Had she for thirty years come to manage their continuous presence while carrying on with her actual life?

In public, I had held firm with the plan, suppressing my obsession so no one could see, doing what my family had done, giving my parents no reason to fight. But I couldn't eradicate those feelings Dad told me to ignore. In bed, at the ballet studio, on the sidewalk to school, images of dead babies ambushed me, flapping up like targets in a penny arcade. I'd try to shove them back, hold them down, keep them from causing trouble. But when the babies spun like tops into the ground, when they flew like witches through black skies, when they crept up through the neck of my shirt and howled, I trembled and grew cold. I flipped on lights, pirouetted with abandon, raced down the pavement, pulling at my skin, joggling my head. Trying to make the torment stop.

So, when my grandmother sat and watched the Dotted Swiss gain dimension, when she connected the dots on the page, I wondered how she couldn't be thinking about her first-born child, despite the years that had passed. I wanted to ask. I always wanted to ask. I looked at her face, her alabaster skin rouged in pink, and I squeezed my eyes like lasers, trying to pierce the manicured veneer and see inside. She had to have had thoughts, if I did. I felt the queasy jolt without having to see the rabbit cage in the garage, and I sensed implicitly that Grandma Lilly suffered similar assaults. But I knew that she was not to be upset, that I wasn't allowed to say anything, not even that I was sorry it happened and wanted to make her feel better. She was to be entertained, kept happy, protected, without ever acknowledging that that was what we were doing. The dictate made me feel anxious and sick, but I toed the line.

She hovered her crayon over the grid, searching for remaining opportunities. "There's always one hiding away, where you just can't see it."

"I think I see one."

"You do? Give me a hint."

"Higher." She moved up the page. "Lower." She moved down. "To the left." We started to giggle. "Now right." Full-on laughter.

She grabbed me with both arms and hugged. "Katie Nichols, you are playing with me."

I smelled the rose-scented powder, felt the sheen of her cardigan against my face. In my mind, my grandparents were still Grandma Lilly and Papa Sam, but they were changed. They were now Grandma Lilly crying by the nursery window and Papa Sam running down the hospital hallway. They were Papa Sam measuring pattern pieces, now the sad man who made party dresses, and Grandma Lilly setting tables with service for eighteen, now the sullen hostess.

Mom worked on the dress during the course of a few weeks, and I tried it on at various points in its construction. I was a diminutive fit model in cotton Carter's underwear, arms straight to the sky and eyes shut as the fabric cascaded over my face, pins scratching my torso and legs as they descended. When Mom was finished, she sat down and inspected the gown for wayward threads or missed stitches, gave it a final press and hung it on a hanger in my closet. It was a beautiful garment, impeccably tailored and elegant.

Sometime before the wedding, Mom lifted the dress off the pole and laid it on the bed. She thought for a moment and left the room. When she returned, she held one of Lill-Dor's oblong cardboard spools, a trail of half-dollar size daisies spilling from its end. Since the gown's completion, my mother had thought that something was missing. It was stunning, yes, but it wasn't distinctive. It wouldn't shift the ethers. It wouldn't outlive the occasion in magnificent ways. This, of course, was the goal of any creative endeavor, or so I was taught. The making of some thing that hadn't been conceived before, that would breach boundaries, that would elicit gasps.

This was the inspiration behind the artistic effort, whatever effort it happened to be. It wasn't enough for a painting to have perspective and color and form, if broken glass rock could be embedded into the pigment. A book report cover could not abide mere construction paper and crayon, if cellophane waterfalls could be superimposed into cut-out windows. If seventh-grade research on the recipes of France could be presented in a baguette basket, each dish written on a bread-shaped slice of card stock. A gown for one's daughter, albeit an exemplary display of workmanship, would not move, inspire, or change the world if it was not adorned, every three inches, in every direction, with embroidered daisies from your father's factory.

My mother cut the chain of flowers into its singular buds and sewed each by hand onto the Dotted Swiss, punching up the staid navy with shots of yellow and white. I felt like a garden. I felt the extraordinary sensation of difference. I felt the weight of the fabric, of family, of obligation.

TEN

IN BALLET, SOME GIRLS could kick their legs up to their shoulders. They didn't have to practice, even. One girl, Jennifer, could hit her nose.

"It's easy," she told us, "you just start with your feet together, like this, and then you lift it up and it just does it."

Her shin literally touched her nostrils.

"You can hurt your face, you know," said Nancy, who could get to her chin, the second-highest. "I wouldn't do that if I were you."

Mine got past my waist, but not much farther. I could kick to the side just fine, keeping my knee perfectly straight and hip tucked, but to the front, my body resisted. The step was supposed to look effortless, as if the leg floated, weightless, hanging at the top and feathering down. At the barre, the more it fought me, the more I pushed. And the more I pushed, the worse the result.

In class the Monday after making the dress with my grandparents, my tepid grand battement was challenged more than usual. Not only did we do double the number of kicks at the barre, they were everywhere in the combination, the short dance we learned in the last third of the lesson. In the middle of the floor, having nothing to hold onto or push off of, they are even harder to do, calling upon abdominal muscles and balance to perform them well. I loved the last third of class, when all the parts merge. The individual movements at the barre, then the traveling steps across the room—they met in the "center," the space where we were untethered and free, where discipline would make room for creativity.

We gathered behind Miss Kellerman to learn the sequence of steps. Right from the start, there were the battements, four of them, with arms to the side and even overhead, and then to make the situation more distressing, développés. The dreaded développés. The slow—painfully slow—raising of pointed toes over the ankle, the calf, to the knee, where they'd press forward and lead the limb into an extension, muscles quivering, foot cramping, face reddening, but everything else still. Unmoving. Développés took strength, flexibility, technique. If my leg hit ninety degrees, it was a good day. Nothing made it feel heavier, less graceful, less balletic.

The first group of dancers, including me, took our spots. Miss Kellerman placed me in front because I never forgot the steps. The music began, and I braced myself in fifth position. A streak of sun pierced my face, and I stayed put, waiting for the count. Miss Kellerman sauntered in front of us, her long pink tutu accenting each stride, her cheeks dusted and eyelids shadowed.

"Three, two, one," she said, clapping.

On the next beat, I thrust my leg out with all that I had, my eyes riveted on the mirror. Then, I stepped forward and kicked the other, hoping to see the bottom of my slipper in the glass. In my peripheral vision, I glimpsed other feet, flashes of gray leather dotting black silhouettes, on stomachs and chests and at the end of the row, Jennifer's nose.

Next were balancés, followed by piqué turns, a chance to move across the floor. I felt my arms succumb to the force of my body, and instead of containing them, I let them do what they pleased as I spun, undisciplined, wild. Miss Kellerman appeared to my side as I slowed for the next two battements, steadying myself, finding my bearings. I threw my foot up, bent and crooked. My hip popped out, and my knee turned in. My chest caved forward. My heart screamed. I kicked and kicked again, and again. Miss Kellerman put her hand on my shoulder and pressed down. "And turn and step," she instructed the other girls while holding on to me. "Glissade, pas de bourrée. Tendu." She took my wrist and extended it to the side, standing behind me, finding my eyes in the mirror. Mine latched onto hers, deep brown, lined in movie-star black. I caught my breath, and with a lift of her chin, a trace of a smile, she folded my arm in front and led me to the next step.

At the door at the end of class, I lined up and waited to leave. I was tired and confused about what had happened or if something happened. When it was my turn, I thought that maybe Miss Kellerman would tell me, but she just nodded and said my name as she always did. I thanked her for class, curtsied and left the studio.

Eleven

Two tall rectangular boxes took up half the floor of the bathroom linen closet. One opened, one in reserve, they stood on their ends under the shelves that held our towels and sheets, sandwiched between extra rolls of toilet paper and a wicker hamper. Nothing in our house came in a box this gigantic. Or this pink.

I had seen the cartons before but didn't think anything of them. They were just big boxes containing some ordinary household item, like the ones for laundry detergent or my father's stationery. But now, drawn into the mystery of my grandparents' past, a lot of what I had been accustomed to seeing became unfamiliar. The junk drawer in the kitchen, with its extra keys. For what? To where? The letters arriving in the mailbox. From whom? Why? I pushed the buttons on the dishwasher, seeing the appliance differently. "Has this always been right here? With this dial? I don't remember the dial." The news, menacing as it was, galvanized my curiosity. I scrutinized everything, and the wonderings ran around my head, chirping like crickets.

One Saturday afternoon when my mother was gardening, I lifted the flap on the open box. On my knees, I tilted it toward me and peered inside. Lined up and stacked like dominoes, white fabric rectangles lay in wait. At first, I thought that they were surgical in nature; in the den, my father kept rolls of gauze in a drawer under the eight-track cassette player. These looked to be made from the same material. Maybe there was not enough room in the drawer.

I took one out. It was thick. Flat strips of gauze extended from the ends. Clearly, the items in the box were not for some routine household purpose. I had never seen them used. They were bandages, extra-thick bandages waiting for some kind of dreadful emergency. The strips would tie around a leg, an arm. Pressure would be applied. Extremity raised over the heart.

I laid the bandage on the floor of the closet and peeled off the exterior layer. With my fingernails, I teased open the padding inside, analyzing the cross-section. The material stayed together and did not fray. This would be a really bad emergency.

I carried the dissected wad to the sink and put it under the faucet. Instantly, it absorbed the trickle of water, so well that I couldn't squeeze it out.

The bathroom door swung open, whacking the linen closet knob behind it.

"What's all this?" My mother scowled and raised her voice, pushing the bandana back on her head. "You're making a flood." She marched to the vanity and shut off the water. "This is not to play with."

I held the dripping pad of gauze in my two hands, fearful now that I had wasted a valuable resource, that a disaster was, in fact, going to occur during my lifetime. "Why do we have so many bandages?"

She grabbed the wet pad from my palms and threw it into the trash can under the sink. I stepped back so the cabinet wouldn't smack my knee.

"You'll need them when you're thirteen. Now clean this all up."

Panic careened through my gut. "What's going to happen when I'm thirteen?"

"It's not important now."

"Does Ben know?"

"It doesn't concern Ben." She lifted up my hand and inspected my fingers. "And what are you doing to your skin? It's all picked off."

I pulled my hand away. "It's not."

"You must stop this. It'll get infected."

She left the bathroom, flipping off the light switch on the way out.

I dried off my fingers, red, now, around the cuticles, and scratched off the tabs of moist skin. I folded back the flaps on the box, pushing the toilet paper and hamper to their original spots. My brother would have a bar mitzvah, and I would bleed to death.

Later, I took Ben into the bathroom and showed him the box. "Have you looked in there?"

"No, why?"

I reached in and pulled out a pad.

He took it from my hand. "Looks like Dad's surgery stuff. What else is in there?" He took out another one. "Wow. So many."

"Mom wouldn't tell me what they're for, but I think it's something very bad, with lots of blood if we have so many. But you don't have to worry, just me."

"That's weird."

"I'm really scared. And she got so mad."

"Let's ask Dad."

We found him on the front porch, sweeping. He couldn't stand a dirty porch. "What do you have there, kiddoes?"

Ben unfolded his hand. "Katie found this. I told her it was one of your surgery things. Right?"

Dad leaned the broom on the wall of the house and drew in a breath.

"It's not, see?" I said.

"Did you ask Mom?"

"She got mad and said I had to wait until I was thirteen, but not Ben. Am I going to have a bad accident or something?"

Dad sat down on a chair. "Okay, no emergencies, no accidents. No one's getting hurt."

"So what are they? And why are there so many?"

"It has to do with the female body. The anatomy."

The screen door squeaked open, and Mom stuck out her head. "Do you want hamburgers or tuna casserole?"

"Hang on a sec, we're having a conversation," Dad said, motioning with his head. "Maybe you want to come out, too."

"Just answer."

He raised his brows, coaxing her.

"Hurry, I've got the sink running."

"Hamburgers."

The door shut. Dad got up and called to her to come back, but she didn't. He explained that boy mammals make sperm, and girl mammals make eggs, and that when they come together, they form a baby. But since they don't make babies all the time, the girls get rid of their extra eggs, and they come out as blood, into the pads, which weren't his bandages for the hospital, after all. And the eggs aren't like the ones in the fridge. And you put the pads in your underwear. And it happens once a month for a couple of days.

"That's gross," Ben said.

"So there's not going to be a war here, like on TV?"

"Of course not," Dad said.

"But blood's going to come out of me when I'm thirteen?" I pressed my fingers to my leg one by one, counting the years.

"Around then, sometimes it's sooner."

Dad looked at my fingertips and said that when I felt like scraping the skin by my nails, I could pick up a crayon or marker and draw a picture instead.

"Keep one in your pocket," he said.

———

While my mother was still in the kitchen, I ran up the steps to her bathroom and grabbed several bunches of pads from the pink box, rolling them in my shirt up to my nipples. Checking both ways first, I crossed the hall into my bedroom, opened my underwear drawer and spilled out the stash.

In front of the dresser, I pulled my underwear down to my knees, pressed a pad between my legs and slid the panties back up, wiggling my thighs and hips and rear end until everything seemed in place. The idea that blood would gush from my body and not hurt like an accident or make me sick or put me on a stretcher was nothing that I could believe. It was horrifying, and it was coming. Soon. I heard steps in the hallway and quickly let down my skirt, shut the drawer and headed to the living room to do something normal.

At the piano, I couldn't catch my breath. I could hardly feel the bench beneath me, levitated as I was by the wad of gauze. It buckled in front. It squeezed my vagina. While playing, it occurred to me that to keep what I was doing under wraps, which seemed like the appropriate thing to do, I'd have to collect my panties right when they came out of the dryer so I could put them back into the drawer myself, and that intercepting them from my mother or Angie in such fashion would likely not be feasible. I slid off the bench, mid-arpeggio, yanked the cotton brick from where it had gotten stuck in my groin and raced up the steps to my room, where I repositioned the remaining stockpile in a floral scarf I used for dress-up, tying it at the corners and hiding it in a woolen beanie instead.

The next morning, and for many mornings to follow, I retrieved a pad from the scarf and inserted it into my underwear before leaving for school. An inch thick and too long for an eight-year-old pelvis, it rubbed against the top of my thighs and rode up in back and front, nearly poking through my panties' elastic waistband. I felt it when I walked, and sat, and simply stood at the blackboard doing multi-digit multiplication. I felt it gripping me, hampering me. But also protecting me. For ballet, though I feared that the jumping and leaping might prompt the blood to shoot out, enthusiastically, I went defenseless, as there was no concealing the bulge under a leotard and tights, and that embarrassment would have been too much to bear. To avoid depleting my mother's supply of menstrual products, I reused the pads I had taken.

On Tuesdays, gym days, we were allowed to wear stretchy shorts under our skirts and dresses. Before class, the girls went into the hall bathroom and pulled them on, which I could do without revealing the mayhem in my underwear. On the third Tuesday after I had begun the pad regimen, we climbed ropes. Previously, I had been able to make it three-quarters of the way to the top, once I got started. Starting was difficult, and it was where everyone could see.

Mr. Milanesi, the gym teacher, stood on the mat and held the rope. He called each kid one at a time and spotted from below, helping him wrap the rope around his ankle, prompting him to pull up his knees and to straighten out, giving a helpful push or lift. Everyone else sat on the floor cross-legged, gazing skyward as if watching a comet. We clapped after each classmate descended. Todd Forrester always jumped on the mat, making the corners kick up with a whoosh.

When it was my turn, I reached my arms as high as I could and grasped the rope. Simultaneously, Mr. Milanesi bent in a squat, preparing to give me a boost on my rear end as he did for nearly all of the girls and some of the boys.

I whipped my head around and looked straight into his horn rims. "I can do it. You don't have to help."

"All right, I'm here if you need me," he said, still squatting.

"I won't, and you can stand up."

He chuckled and stood straight.

I pulsed my knees in preparation and counted to three, jumping up, my legs searching for the rope, my face straining. I let go and tried again.

This time, Mr. Milanesi coiled the rope around my foot. I felt his shoulder graze my hip, and I kicked, unraveling the cable, flying down to the mat, pressing down my dress.

"Don't help," I said. My hands burned, and I felt hot. Some kids giggled.

I faced the rope again and closed my eyes, willing myself to attach magnetically and slide to the heavens, defying gravity and fear and blood and menstrual pads. *Mind over matter*, Dad had said.

I checked to see that Mr. Milanesi had backed off, and I sprung up again, my legs flailing but finding the rope this time. I swung, maneuvering it around one ankle and pinching it with my other foot. Breathless, I had to scamper fast. I raised my knees along the rope, squeezing it to keep it in place, ascending, but not out of Mr. Milanesi's reach. A breeze wafted as I swayed, lifting my dress, and I reached around with one hand to push it down, leaving just the other to hold my sixty-two pounds. The rope fibers dug into my palm, the pain penetrating as I began to slip. Hanging in the balance, fearing both a fall and certain exposure, I felt my menstrual pad shift and wobble, compressed between Mr. Milanesi's hand and me. It shot me up like a rocket, and I clutched the rope with my free hand and wriggled my body yard after yard, burn after burn, until there was nowhere else to go.

After school that day, my mom got a phone call from my teacher, Mrs. Colson.

"You're kidding," I heard her say. "Are you sure?"

I lingered in the kitchen to listen. Mom stared at me, her face contorted.

"Well, I will get to the bottom of it," she said, hanging up.

She walked over to me and patted me from behind. "You're not wearing the pads from my bathroom closet, are you?"

A pang reverberated in my chest.

"The ones you were playing with. Are you wearing them to school?"

I didn't know what to say.

"Mrs. Colson said you wouldn't come down from the rope. Why would you do that?"

I rubbed my hands, still chafed.

She sat me on her lap. "You're eight. You have a long time. You don't need them yet."

"Dad said it could happen before I'm thirteen."

"Maybe twelve and a half. Wear them when you're twelve and a half."

TWELVE

"YOU SURE YOU WANT to keep this thing?" Angie asked, holding the jar at arm's length.

I took it from her and put it back on my bookshelf.

"Whose is it anyway?" she said, "that brain in there."

I spun the container. "A sheep. Look, this is where I sliced it."

Angie winced. "Child, it's grisly. Get that away from me."

On Saturday mornings, I went to a science class for exceptional boys and girls. The dissection was to teach us about the structure of the sheep's brain, which is similar to that of a human being. Once we learned about the parts of the organ, we could understand how it works. I was nine. I was taking Anatomy. My father was euphoric.

If my mother nurtured my creativity, my father commandeered my own gray matter. He cultivated my thinking. Demanding, unrelenting and impatient when it came to accomplishment, he had techniques for stretching my scholastic abilities to their limits. Some were outright dictates—you will take this class and get this grade. Others were couched in compassion and sugar—perhaps, baby girl, you'd like to invite Janey over after the planetarium.

I knew what he was doing. I felt the angst, the squeeze. But I trusted him. A child can do this. She can endure the constraints when she believes the motive. In my case, the motive was to be the best at something, and my father had convinced me that I, in fact, could be that. It was not vapid inspirational talk. It was not an unfulfilled adult on the sidelines. It was not for him. A selfless man, my father truly thought that I had what it took, or he thought that what I had would take me to the top.

I fell for his assessment, inspired by his thinking that I could do it, whatever it turned out to be. I tolerated the tough, sweetened up with outings to The Checkerboard for ices and permission to style his hair in barrettes and bows, because he explained to me why it was important. Learning was a desperate act. Excelling, a moral imperative. Without it, we'd crumble. We'd all crumble. I was part of some greater societal effort, beyond my own achievement, and I was all in. I had fun cutting up the sheep's brain. I idolized my father and wanted him to be proud. And, the concrete process of shaving a sliver of the organ and seeing exactly, definitively, what was hidden inside of it was particularly satisfying at that moment, when I was realizing that so much of life couldn't be carved up and viewed under a microscope. So much of it was a secret.

My father was raised with the purpose that he instilled in Ben and me. Unlike Lilly and Sam, his parents, Leo and Sofie, didn't have sets of china for eighteen, or even twelve, complete with fish forks and gravy boats, and they didn't grow up with closets of crinolines or the sensibility that would support them. They did have books and opinions and a little yellow house a block from the ocean in Long Island, having made their way from what is now Ukraine, to Boston and ultimately, Atlantic Beach, New York, not far from where my mother lived as a child.

Leo left the town of Rovno in 1913, at eighteen, in between the Russian Revolutions, just a year before the start of World War One. His family had experienced the Tsar's discrimination of minorities, low wages, and prohibition from owning land, voting and attending school. Before emigrating, he was caught up in an uprising that left many of his neighbors dead. In 1941, a German firing squad murdered eighteen thousand Rovno Jews. The town's five thousand surviving residents were put into a ghetto and exterminated in 1942.

Leo was a harness maker as a teenager in Russia. In Boston, where he and Sofie married, he learned how to upholster furniture and later, he managed several residential properties in his neighborhood.

Sofie, too, fled western Russia for the U.S. at around the same time, becoming a writer for a newspaper. Her column addressed the issues facing women of the day. Nana Sofie had sass.

The yellow house on Daytona Street had a front porch, where my grandmother would often be when we drove up for a visit. She had Parkinson's Disease and couldn't move around too well, but she hugged me hard with both arms, pulling me into her chest as she sat, looking up into my face. My grandfather, robust and energetic, climbed on ladders, repaired the house, cooked. Fair-skinned and blue-eyed, he burned in the sun, as did my dad. Inside the house, a chessboard was set on a wooden table. He and my father spoke about current events and politics and more practical concerns, too, while they played. Sometimes, Grandpa Leo spoke in English, sometimes in Yiddish, which my father understood. Ben and I watched, tried to learn the game and giggled at the funny words. We never stayed too long, but we did walk to the beach and explore the house, filled as it was with humble furnishings, a few knick-knacks here and there. Nothing was polished or shiny. Nothing seemed new. But the home contained the essentials, and my grandparents were comfortable in it.

A month after my cousin's wedding, his parents, my Aunt Eleanor and Uncle Roger, stopped at the house one Saturday when we were visiting. They lived nearby in a heavy stone tudor tangled in ivy. Aunt Eleanor, who was about five years older than my dad, taught high school French and wore cat-eye sunglasses and leopard print coats. Several evenings a week, she swam laps at the YMCA, often as many as fifty. She gave me a book off her shelf each time we saw her, along with her assessment of the characters, most of whom were young girls. Heidi, the Little Women, Pippi Longstocking.

Eleanor entered carrying groceries, her Lauren Bacall bob wild from the coastal wind. She set down the bags when she saw Ben and me. "Twice in a month. Am I a lucky auntie."

Everyone greeted her and Roger except for my mother, who stayed put in a chair she'd been attached to for the previous hour, a needlepoint project draping her lap. Even Nana Sofie got up and made her way across the room, with Leo's help. Mom pulled in her feet as they passed, keeping her head cast down, her fingers pulling stitches, her mouth shut. She didn't speak with Leo and Sofie that day, not even to make simple small talk.

When Eleanor walked inside, my mother twisted in the chair and groaned, loud enough to hear.

Dad tensed up like a soldier and pressed his lips together, hard. "Ignore it," he told his sister. Grandpa Leo said something in Yiddish.

Uncle Roger took the bags into the kitchen. "Ben, Kate, come help me with these."

While we put apples and carrots into the refrigerator, I saw my parents through the door that led to the living room. Dad bent at the waist, leaning over my mother, talking fast, reddening. His forearms shot up and cut the air like knives. His legs shifted weight; his feet stomped. She didn't look at him, just waved him off with her palm.

I didn't know why my mother was rude in my grandparents' home, why she muttered under her breath and made negative remarks. It was beginning to feel futile asking her the reasons for things; she rarely answered directly and if she did, her explanations left me worn out and insecure. It was not the first time that she had been inconsiderate to Grandpa Leo and Nana Sofie, but I hadn't seen such arguing before. Perhaps, my mother's decision to tell me about the dead baby wasn't the only threat to their happiness. I sensed that my ability to control the outcome was slipping away.

On top of all that, I felt bad for my grandparents. I hated my mother's behavior, not merely because I knew that incivility was unacceptable. What disturbed me was that the person who was supposed to show me how to be in the world had made me doubt that I could trust her. She was supposed to make me feel stronger and safer, but she had created confusion. She had even caused me to wonder if I shouldn't like my grandparents, too. Catching myself, I felt awful for having the thought, understanding the betrayal of loyalty imposed upon my affection. But I couldn't follow her lead or excuse her actions, even at nine. I loved my grandparents, and I loved my father, and I gave him the devotion that I was not willing to give my mother. I was a pint-sized Lady Justice, without the robe.

Our visits were an opportunity for my father to check on his parents, particularly his mom, whom he examined. He took her pulse, listened to her heart with the stethoscope that he brought from home, asked her to hold out her arms and rotate them out and in, press down hard and then up. Grandma Sofie concentrated, pursing her lips, grunting while she pushed, watching her son watch her. After the evaluation, she smiled, maybe because she was happy it was over, maybe because she was proud. My father's expression was consistent, regardless of his assessment of her condition.

I had begun to see that apart from the two ends of the emotional curve—anger and supreme joy—feelings weren't obvious on my father's face or shared with his words. He seldom said, I am happy, I am worried, I am sad. He said that the operating room had trained him to be cool, calm and collected, The Three C's. Outside of that singular chamber, at home with us, it gave me the impression of equilibrium, reliability, fortitude. It also made his infrequent waverings, like the one in my grandparents' living room, that much more potent. I became an astute observer of his twinges, a pull of the upper lip, a crinkling of the cheek, a flicker of the eye. The slightest difference in his outward expression registered with me, and I read each one like a ticker tape from his soul. I felt an umbilical connection to his psyche, positioned as I was at the end of a silent and privileged conduit. I believed that no one understood him as well as I did. With mounting indications that he and my mother were treacherously different people, I paid extra attention.

Before we were to leave Atlantic Beach that Saturday afternoon, Ben said that he was hungry. Quickly, Grandpa Leo whipped up a hamburger on the stove, and while I have no idea what he seasoned it with, the aroma—of garlic? Pepper? Paprika?—was nothing that I had smelled in our kitchen. Though I had declined the offer for a snack when it was first made, something in my expression registered with my grandfather, who ran out to our car after we had said good-bye, pulled open the back door, reached over my brother and handed me a steaming, savory, glorious burger of my own, cradled in a slice of folded rye.

My mother turned in her seat. "Don't make a mess."

Grandpa Leo stood on the sidewalk in trousers and a plaid shirt. Work shoes. My dad's barrel chest. I peeled one palm off of the sandwich and waved to him out the window, ribbons of spice circling me like a top, unraveling in the beach air.

THIRTEEN

ON THE FOLLOWING WEEKEND, the annual recital of The Miss Kellerman School of Dance went off without a hitch. The performance was an exhilarating success. Immediately after our exit from the stage, my classmates and I ascended the staircase, turned left into the older girls' dressing room, slipped off our costumes and ran into the hall in relevé, our arms criss-crossed over our bare prepubescent chests. We were permitted inside the hallowed teenage chamber only on this day, one hour and fifteen minutes before the recital, when we found our names pinned to the waists of our tutus and whisked them off the poles, and immediately following our curtsy, to return the costumes to the racks. Entering the room was breaching a sanctum, a hideaway for adolescent empresses outfitted with secret cabinets and mirrors, waves of tulle skirts on the walls, swooping above us like garlands.

I found my bag in the hallway and pulled on my dress, jostling for space with my classmates, all of us giddy from the show. We had worn sky blue tutus and pink tights, which I kept on under my sandals. They were thinner than the black ones we wore in class, and they felt satiny and luxurious. I went downstairs and out to the garden behind the house, where Miss Kellerman was hosting the yearly reception, her pink punch in a crystal bowl and sugar cookies piled high on silver trays. It was a northeastern June Saturday, dry and sunny. The stone patio was filled with parents and siblings standing in groups, each with its own ballerina, her hair still in a bun and makeup intact. I spotted my family by the edge of the fountain, where a little boy was tossing a penny.

"There she is," Ben called. Mom had made him dress up in a sports coat.

She pressed her cheek up against mine. "The most gorgeous."

"Yes, Katie, you really are something," said Dad, squeezing my hand.

"How do you spin so many times in a row?" Ben asked.

I was still thinking about the performance, hearing the music, counting the beats. I felt my body mark the movements involuntarily. My leg stretched behind me in tendu, my arm curved in first position. My neck elongated, and I looked out at the crowd, the audience.

Dad handed me a glass of punch. "Looks like Miss Kellerman is coming to say hello."

I straightened up and tucked my hips.

"Dr. and Mrs. Nichols," she said, lowering her chin to each. "And Kate, you danced beautifully today. I am very proud of you."

It was odd to see Miss Kellerman in a dress and high heels.

"I've seen a new strength this year, a new intensity, especially lately," she told my parents, drawing out the words.

"She just loves it, don't you, Katie?" my mother said. "She really can't wait to get to class."

I saw Miss Kellerman smile carefully at Dad, squinting slightly. Strength and intensity would be good things for her to have seen, but Dad didn't say, "Fantastic," or "Terrific," in that brisk cadence, as he normally would have. He looked tentative, as if Miss Kellerman was transmitting a different message.

"It's very...passionate." Then, as she had appeared, she whisked away, her circle skirt churning at her calves.

Ben and I filled a plate with cookies, and I introduced him to a couple of my friends. Beyond the table, I saw my father talking again with Miss Kellerman. He nodded his head, pressing a hand under his chin before hurrying back across the lawn.

"What did she say to you?" I asked him at the end of the party, while we walked around the side of the house to the car.

"Oh, I had a question for her. Nothing important."

Mom always planned a special dinner after the recital and invited my four grandparents. Miss Kellerman's studio wasn't big enough for extra spectators, so each year, they came to our house, and I danced for them in the living room.

Unless some issue of national security intervened, Grandma Lilly arrived holding a white box in front of her chest. On our front step, she pinched the red-and-white bakery string with her fingers, their polished pink tips an upside-down tulip. Inside the box, my brother and I hoped, was the Black Forest Cake and not the Apple Crumb Pie. For this recital dinner, she indeed brought the cake, topped with a plastic ballerina in arabesque. Leo and Sofie rang the bell a few minutes later, carrying a tin of homemade potato salad. As kids do, Ben and I brought all of our grandparents together for such occasions. With her own parents present, I hoped that my mother would let Leo and Sofie be, but I couldn't be sure that she would. My stomach was a skein of yarn.

I took the potatoes into the kitchen, where Angie was checking the oven. She lifted the corner of the foil and peeked inside. "Mmm, I smell pickles in these."

"They're Russian, that's why."

She took the tin from me and set it in the fridge. "I may have to steal the recipe."

"Can I help do anything?"

"Not today, it's your day." She smoothed the collar on my dress. "Now go on and see your grandfolks."

"Come in fifteen minutes. That's when the show starts."

"Wouldn't miss it."

In the living room, Lilly sat in front of the picture window, which Mom had outfitted with extravagant cornices covered in silver and white wallpaper. They were cut into wide arches that dropped to the shocking pink carpet, an homage to Versailles, by way of Athens, by way of Greenwich Village. Lilly wore a pastel pantsuit and flats, hair pulled up, teased and sprayed into a bouffant. Still chestnut, the style lent a studied and regal air, and it set off her flawless pale skin, translucent in New Rochelle's afternoon sun.

Leo helped Sofie into an armchair, holding her by the arm as she found the seat under her and placing her purse on the carpet. She looked older than she was, wrinkles lining her forehead, the skin under her arms dangling. Because of the Parkinson's, she didn't fuss with makeup or hair color, choosing a natural wash-and-wear style that she could maintain herself. Some years later, I found a photograph of my dad that she had cut in half, excising her own image.

"She was self-conscious," he said.

"Are there any pictures of her?"

"Only from before."

Sofie adjusted the top of her floral dress and clapped her hands, beaming. "On with the show," she said, a tremor in her voice. "Prima ballerina."

Ben worked the cassette player, and everyone else took their seats. I began off-stage, out of the room, and entered when he hit Play. I performed the recital dance, feeling freer in my movements on the hot pink carpet than on the studio hardwoods. My leaps felt higher, my turns quicker. I lost restraint and tension in my muscles and my mind. My legs soared skyward; my arms became ribbons, all traces of bone and cartilage having evaporated. I hardly knew where I was. The music ended, and I wound out of a spin, and another, coming to a final pose in silence, breathless. I walked to the center of the stage, stepped to the side on my right leg, bent the left behind and curtsied. Everybody sat still, staring. My mother clapped. Grandma Sofie cried. Ben jumped up and tossed a beaded flower at my feet.

We sat around the dining table, and I looked at my relatives, passing roasted turkey and spinach soufflé and Grandpa Leo's pickled potatoes, and I saw through them to their histories. A Russian village with goats and horses. A row house garment factory on Manhattan's Lower East Side. And now this, me, here.

It was six months after I learned about the baby, and his tragic little life was now embedded in my family's story. Like my great-grandmother Beatrice, who saved chicken fat in a jar and used it to fry onions until they were black. Who stabbed herself with the insulin she kept in a cigar box. Or like the circus and the zoo that my mother was kept from, for fear the animals would break from their restraints and devour her whole. The tale of the infant was fixed in our lineage, meaning something, though I couldn't yet know what. And the disruption that it caused was also lodged in me. I was regimented, yes, and I could follow a pattern, whether made from tissue paper and pinned onto fabric or imposed by decree. I could tell myself to squelch emotions and rely on my temporal lobe. But I was young, and the practice hadn't been drummed into me long enough for it to take hold completely, to become a second skin.

"A toast," said Grandpa Leo.

I snapped to the present. Everyone lifted a glass.

"To our magnificent ballerina, congratulations. May your stages become bigger and bigger."

In between dinner and dessert, I went upstairs to take off my tights. Everyone had gone outside to the patio, except for Mom and Angie, who were putting the food away and doing the dishes. On my way back down, I heard my parents in the kitchen.

Dad's voice was quiet, and his words were slow. "She asked me what was going on at home."

"Why would she ask that?"

I stopped on the steps and held the banister.

"She didn't say, exactly, but…"

"But what?"

"It's the intensity. She thinks it's too much, that something's eating at her."

I wasn't sure who they were talking about, but I kept listening.

"Because she loves to dance?" my mother said. "That's crazy. I've taught hundreds of kids."

"Did you watch her? It's like she's hypnotized, or spooked."

I got closer to the door and pressed my ear to the wall.

Dad waited before speaking again. "She hasn't been herself. She seems preoccupied, anxious."

I didn't like being talked about this way, analyzed without my knowing. A brain in a jar.

"I don't see that."

"Jesus, of course. Damn it," my father said, startling me. "I thought she was okay."

"What are you talking about?"

"It's what you told her, about your brother. It's got to be."

"Oh, please."

"How you could do that I'll never understand."

I shivered against the wall.

"Leave me alone already, will you? And you, of all people, should talk about babies."

"Keep your voice down."

Angie stepped lightly out of the kitchen and closed the louver doors behind her, turning into the living room without seeing me.

"We agreed to never bring that up," my father said.

"Don't blame me, then."

Cabinets banged shut. Drawers opened and closed.

My father's pitch rose. "Have you forgotten what it could do to us?"

I tore down to the landing, through the den and into the garage. Angie heard and called to me, following me, but I kept moving. In seconds, I was on my bike, peeling out of the driveway, past the Brants' house, the willow tree, the hydrant that marked our finish lines. I pumped my legs and gripped the handlebars, sweaty, trembling, nauseated. The saliva came first, filling in behind my teeth, tasting of potatoes. Of pickles, mayonnaise. I heard myself moaning, then shrieking, then retching, and I kept pedaling, covering myself in vomit, not sure where I would end up.

My parents would soon be in the car, looking for me, calling my name into the persimmon sky, fearing the dark. I turned onto Mulberry and wove around a web of roads behind the school. They would have choices for where to turn, and I hoped they would choose wrong. I rode through the neighborhood, past houses of kids from my class, windows lit gold. Susan Harmon's and Billy Sloate's backed up to each other, and a path ran alongside the double yard. It was lined with forsythia, and it was off the street. My tires bounced on the stones and crunched to a stop. I crouched between the bushes and the bike and sat on the dirt, sickened by the smell of my dress and despite the impending dark, not at all afraid.

———

The policemen found me several hours later, sleeping under the yellow branches. They stood over me, pointing flashlights at my face. My parents rushed from behind them and descended onto my body, stroking my head, trying to scoop me from the ground.

"Oh my god, Katie, Katie..." my mother sobbed, flopping onto me.

Dad dropped to a knee. "Let's get you home."

I sat up and pushed them away.

One of the policemen held out a hand.

I stood by myself, saying nothing. The four of them watched. The second policeman picked up my bike. My mother tried to touch me again. She was shaking. I didn't care.

I looked at her, quivering on the path, and at my father, his hand on her shoulder. Last I encountered them, they were arguing. Now he was touching her.

"We'll wait until you're ready to go," the first policeman said. Sgt. Paul Oliver. The moon found the gold nameplate on his chest.

I looked at Sgt. Paul Oliver. It wasn't his fault. My skin itched, having been fed upon by mosquitoes. I put one foot in front of the other and proceeded to the street, where the Bonneville was parked behind the squad car. My father opened the back door.

"We'll take the bike and follow you home," the second policeman said.

I stood by the police car, instead. Surprised, Sgt. Oliver looked at my father for permission. My mother exploded in tears, as if I had been mauled by a bear.

I got in. There were a lot of lights on the dashboard. They loaded my blue Schwinn into the trunk and spoke to someone on the radio, saying they had found the "missing person."

"How long was I a missing person?" I asked.

"A couple hours," said Sgt. Paul Oliver, looking at me in the mirror.

I took it in, the passing of time. I felt missing. "I'm sorry I don't smell very good."

They drove by the front of Billy Sloate's house, and a few minutes later, they parked in front of mine. My parents were waiting by the curb.

"Thank you," I said.

Sgt. Paul Oliver flipped on the ceiling light and looked straight at me. "It's dangerous at night. Try not to run out again, okay?"

I nodded and got out.

My mother moved toward me, clenching her hands. "Why wouldn't you drive with us? Why did you run away? What is wrong with you?"

I avoided her and said nothing. My father tried to quiet her down.

Inside, Ben and Angie were waiting on the steps in the foyer. It was after eleven o'clock, but they were still up. Ben looked stunned and exhausted. He probably wanted to ask me where I hid and whether I peed in the grass. He probably wanted to say that he couldn't believe it, any of it, but Angie had told him not to.

"I'm glad you're back," he said, on cue, looking past me and out the window. "You went in the squad car?"

Angie put her hand on my shoulder and walked with me up the steps and into the hall bath, where she rolled up the hem of my dress all the way to the top, lifting it carefully over my head so the dried vomit wouldn't get on my face. She took out the pins from my bun, still tight and secure, and she unraveled my hair with her fingers.

"Step in," she said, checking the temperature of the water. "And just stand under it. No rush."

Angie had never run a bath for me or turned on a shower, even when I was younger and needed help. That was my mother's domain. I stood under the water and let it pour down on me, taking with it the hairspray and mascara, the dirt and the stench, but not the dismay. When I was finished, Angie held open a towel and I moved into it, water dripping from my lashes, my ears, my fingertips. I stood on the mat, swaddled, her steady hands stroking my back.

FOURTEEN

I WOKE UP THE next morning, Sunday, and went into the kitchen. My father had already returned from rounds at the hospital and was waiting for me in his chair, across from mine, still wearing a tie. I took the box of Black Forest Cake out of the refrigerator and snatched a fork from the drawer.

My mother came in from the yard, holding two four-inch cucumbers and one shrunken pepper. "Look at these measly things. Some harvest."

My parents looked like strangers. Secrets can do this; they can alter a walk, a shape of the mouth, posture. They can elicit odd expressions, peculiar sounds, entrances into rooms.

I stood at the counter and opened the box. No one had touched the cake. I ratcheted back in time and remembered that it was before dessert that I had changed out of my tights and stopped on the steps and heard life-shifting talk that would disrupt the way I saw my parents, my family, me. That would again shatter everything that I believed was true. That would swipe the trust I had in my father, the stability I got from my father, in one tenuous swoop.

So, no, no one ate the cake. I inserted the fork into the whole of it and pulled off bite after bite, licking the icing from the tines and doing it again, making the entire cake mine. It was my recital, after all. It was my ruined night, life, existence. It would be my cake, with my saliva stuck back into it after each swallow. Did she really think I would converse about a pepper?

I left the room, and I left my parents, having uttered no words about anything.

There were four weeks left of school before summer vacation. I had homework to do for Monday, a diorama about the supreme god of the Chickasaw Indian tribe, Ababilini. He represented the four things in the atmosphere that the tribe revered, which they aptly named the Four Beloved Things Above—the Sun, Clouds, Clear Sky and He That Lives in the Clear Sky. I supposed that He was Ababilini himself and figured that the Chickasaws really must have cherished Him if he was on such an esteemed list of Things. I had planned to create his figure out of the Sun, Clouds and Clear Sky, using yellow fabric and fringe, white pillow stuffing and turquoise paint, and fly him in the shoebox over a stream. Additionally, it seemed that when they fished, the men in the Chickasaw village made a deep hole in the river bed into which they inserted a poison that the fish would eat, making them groggy and easier to spear when they floated to the surface. I thought I'd place some construction paper men by the water's edge and if possible, have one hold up a drugged carp in his hand. I didn't like Ababilini, thinking him to be pretentious about his status in the community, and I really despised the fishermen for their insidious hunting and gathering methods. I intended to title the whole art project, "Why I Hate The Chickasaws."

But I decided not to do the assignment, or any of my other homework. This was a time for rebellion. Besides the running away, there was not much more in my power that I could do. I couldn't drive to Virginia in the Bonneville or smoke cigarettes. There weren't bad kids to hang out with in elementary school. I couldn't do drugs like the hippies. The state of things—the Things Above My Little World—was frustrating. All that was at my disposal was my parents' expectations. So, I would smash them. I'd make my mother and father think that I was useless and would amount to nothing. This, they would feel viscerally, having invested so much hope in my success. They would want to run out of the house, aghast, strung along and let down. They would want to hide under a yellow bush while night came, not a care in their souls for whom they might worry.

Not much earlier, I had determined to be a model of perfection in order to keep my parents together, and now, I was preparing to be a failure to keep myself in one piece. The whole thing confounded me, but what else could I do?

I left my bedroom and sat on the swing in the backyard. Ben came out through the sliding doors.

He picked up a football and tossed it to himself, one hand to the other. "Where'd you go, anyway?"

"Around."

"Mom and Dad went nuts."

I walked the swing back and waited before jumping on. "What did they say to you?"

"Something like you heard them arguing, and it must have upset you."

I sailed forward, extending my legs, and back, tucking them under, several times before stopping abruptly. "That's not why." I stared straight at Ben. "They have a secret."

He caught the ball and pulled it into his chest. "What are you talking about?"

"I heard them in the kitchen yelling about how it would be bad if people found out."

"Found out what? That's crazy."

"I don't know what, but Dad got really mad because Mom was never supposed to say anything. We have to find out what it is."

"Just ask them."

"They're not going to tell. When people hide things, they don't all of a sudden tell you about them. And there's something else. Grandma Lilly had a baby who fell off a cart in the hospital and died, and we can't ask anything because it will upset her."

His face went white. "You're making this stuff up."

"I am not. It's true. Mom said."

"It can't be true. You didn't hear right." He swatted his hand in the air. "Then why didn't you tell me?"

"I tried, but Mom said not to."

"So she had a brother, that's what you're saying."

I nodded. "Everything is messed up."

I told him about how I knew and how I had nightmares and how

I lied to him about cleaning the erasers for Mrs. Colson. I said that I almost told him when we walked home from school but couldn't disobey because I never disobeyed. I told him about The Checkerboard and that Dad was mad at Mom for scaring me and how I heard them arguing when I was in bed, trying to fall asleep. Ben just sat and listened, and he seemed dazed and sad about these things, these strange and catastrophic things that we hadn't encountered before in our sweet little lives. These complications and doubts, these questions of truth and motivation. These circumstances that made our parents not just our parents, but other people walking around in the world doing things that had nothing to do with raising us and feeding us and making us feel secure, or at least that's how it felt to me.

We were nine and ten. We had no answers. We could only react and choose what to believe to feel okay. Ben chose to believe that my parents kept nothing from us that we needed to know and shouldn't be challenged. I wasn't so sure. I was done hiding how I felt. I needed to know everything.

———————

My mother called us for lunch. I took my time getting to the kitchen. Everyone else had started eating. Tuna sandwiches and salad, tomato soup. A place had been set for me.

Dad looked up when I walked in. "Soup's getting cold. Come sit."

I stood in front of the refrigerator and took out the Black Forest Cake, again, and an apple and a handful of turkey, which I grabbed from its white paper package.

We were taught to hold our utensils delicately, take small bites and put our napkins on our laps the moment after sitting. We did not speak while chewing. We did not reach to retrieve an olive from a dish or a roll from a basket. We knew that you served from the left and cleared from the right.

I kicked the fridge shut with my bare foot, stuck a fork into my mouth and carried the items out of the kitchen to the den, turkey clenched in my palm.

"That's it," my father said, his chair scraping the floor.

I continued down the steps to the marigold couch and turned on the TV, dialing up the volume.

He marched into the room right behind me and smacked the knob. I sat on the sofa, the cake box on my lap, biting off the turkey that hung from my fist.

"I don't know what you're doing, but it's enough," he said, planted on the shag rug, elbows jutting from his waist. "If you're mad, your job is to figure out why and then handle it properly. Not like this. Not with danger and irresponsibility."

He whisked the cake from my lap and snatched the apple off the couch. "Put that on top of the box," he said, throwing his head at the turkey, "and follow me."

My father had a signature gait, a subtle slapping of the foot upon impact. A slight turn-in, maybe three-quarters of a centimeter. He walked at a clip across the terrazzo into the foyer and up the steps, hitting every other one as he always did, even while balancing my lunch in his hands. My insurrection in his hands. I got up slowly and did as he said.

"Wash up." He motioned to the sink. "And sit down."

Ben and my mother were still at the table. Ben took a bite of his sandwich, chewing carefully and anticipating the impending beat-down. He appeared eager, blinking his curly-lashed eyes, shifting focus from one parent to the other. When they disciplined one of us, they kept the other close by. Information is power. Birds and stones.

I pulled out the chair and sat in a slouch. My father waited. Ben froze.

"For Christ's sake, sit straight, now," my mother said, setting her glass down hard.

I shifted in my seat and crossed my arms.

My father placed both palms flat on the table. "Why don't you tell us why you're so angry."

Ben's eyes begged me.

I analyzed my options. I could answer my father's question, as I had always answered his questions, in a methodical and serious fashion. He would listen carefully, whether he agreed with what I said or not. And if he disagreed, he would try to sway my thinking, but only if the issue at hand had consequences. That's how I learned about priorities. So, I didn't feel ambushed or fear judgment. I just wasn't sure if I wanted to stop rebelling yet. Breaking rank felt powerful. I could defy one simple expectation—sitting down at the table for a sandwich—and launch a series of emotions, thoughts and responses in two competent adults. I could cause them to worry about my sanity and my judgment, let alone their own ability to raise me according to plan. Rebelling was vicious. It was exhilarating. But it was also lonely.

I wanted to punish my parents for keeping things from me, but sitting at the table, tomato soup waiting on my daisy placemat, I also felt tired and alienated and despondent, sentiments that would typically send me to my parents for support and to my father, in particular, for guidance. I relied on him to structure and organize my life, and with this, this fractured trust, that was now shattered.

Dad had trained me in my short nine years to make unemotional decisions. He hadn't yet taught me how to trust my instincts. Perhaps I was too young to have reliable ones, and he was waiting until I had matured to dispense that lesson. Perhaps he was too much a man of science to ever concede to them. That day in the kitchen, I did the rational thing.

I turned toward my mother. "You told Dad he shouldn't talk about babies, and he said you weren't supposed to bring it up. Ever."

She swallowed.

My father didn't blink.

For all of my telepathic sensitivity regarding his emotional state, I couldn't detect a flutter on his face, not a quiver, not a microscopic twitch. I tapered my gaze. Nothing.

"She did say that, yes, but..." He grabbed his chin.

"Why did you run out of the house and hide all night?" my mother yelled. "You scared us to death."

"She thinks you have secrets," Ben said, done with being patient.

My parents went silent.

"Is that what you think?" my father asked.

"You have a secret about some baby. You're not supposed to have secrets."

Mom got up to get the water pitcher.

Dad put down his spoon.

"What baby were you talking about? And why did you yell at each other like that?"

"That was nothing that had to do with you." Dad clasped his hands. "And I'm sorry it upset you."

Ben leaned across the table. "See? I told you."

"But you said it would be bad for our family, so why can't we know?"

"I don't have to know anything," said Ben.

My parents caught eyes, and I detected an infinitesimal shake of my dad's head. A directive.

"Our family is fine, and some things are not for children's ears."

"But my ears heard already, so just tell me. Please, just tell me."

My father brushed back his hair and cleared his throat. He looked pained, twisting in the chair. He took extra time to speak. "Another family, people you don't know, asked me to help them with something."

"Who? And what did they ask you?"

My mother nodded as my father spoke, glancing at him sideways. She was nodding too much.

"That is all you need to know. And we're all safe and sound." He forced a smile, a misshapen and quivering rectangle that couldn't contain the words spewing from them.

I heard breaths escape between his rows of teeth. I saw sweat on his temple. I saw that he needed to be done with this, that he was agonizing over something, a sight I hadn't witnessed and one that did not look or feel good. I had believed him implicitly before, and now, I had to believe that there was a legitimate reason for him to hold on to whatever it was that he was concealing. I sensed, without a doubt, that there was something being hidden, but my father was conveying to me that my knowledge of it would be far worse than the omission. I had no choice but to trust him, even though I didn't know what I was trusting. I picked up my sandwich and took a bite, the essence of loyalty smacking me in the head. "All right."

His eyelids blinked shut, a half-second too long. His chest stretched full. I slid from my seat and hugged him around his neck, where aftershave and antiseptic collided, rising up like vapor from the sea.

FIFTEEN

"LET'S PAINT," MY MOTHER said a few hours later. "I want to make a new lady."

From a stiff poster board, Mom had cut out a three-foot high human form, seated in profile, its back rounded, legs pulled in. She surrounded it with other abstract shapes that dovetailed the subject's perimeter in certain places and jutted out elsewhere. On a table in our basement, she played with their positioning, sliding the pieces in silence, a magician manipulating cards. Once certain, she picked up the largest shape, the woman, and flipped her over onto sheets of newspaper.

Laid out like a bather at the beach, she waited while Mom mixed her paints. Months later, these tubes of oils would squeeze out impressionistic landscapes and jaunty bouquets, but this printmaking constituted Mom's modern phase. Her 1960s homage. She gripped the Brayer roller and ran it over her spots of paint, grabbing several different shades at once and depositing them on the body, layering, building, creating depth and shadow in reverse.

"Now you try," she said. "Mix a little pink with the orange, maybe. Then we'll flip it onto the paper and press."

I dipped the rubber roller into the colors on the palette and dabbed them onto the woman's belly. Mom showed me where to put streaks of pale peach, where the sun would light her up. When it was time, we lifted the shape, sailed it high and rotated it, before lowering it onto the parchment below. The painting smoothed the prior unrest. It was a return to normalcy that quieted me, physically, despite the lingering secret. Like a trance, the lifting of the pigment, the rolling, the pressing, slowed my heart rate, settled my stomach, for the moment, anyway. But nothing was as it was before, though I now had to convince myself that it was. I wasn't sure if I could.

The first printed woman, shaded in purples and grays, hung in our den. She had cousins, rolled out in greens for a friend, blues for my father's office. This pastel incarnation was headed for Neptune Avenue, a birthday present for Grandma Lilly.

"Ready to see?" Mom asked.

She pressed her fingertips to the sides of the poster board, one shape at a time. "I'm going to peel them off, so you hold down the paper."

I peeked under the forms as Mom lifted them, taken by the emergence of new colors and the precision of the edges. This pink lady, though born of a pattern, was her own person.

"She's the most beautiful one," I said. "Grandma's going to love her."

Mom laid the cut-outs on the floor to dry. "You know, she was pretty worried about you when you ran away."

The words pelted me in the gut and hovered in the basement air. I hadn't considered my grandparents, in all this time.

"They know you're okay now." Mom ripped off the palette paper and tossed it out. "You can call them on the phone if you want."

I was supposed to protect Grandma Lilly, but instead, I made her afraid again. I held onto the edge of the table.

"They're fine now, don't worry."

Mom pulled me into her chest and kissed my head. The lunchtime conversation consumed my thoughts. In my limited experience with family mysteries, I believed that they all had something to do with infants. I was sick of infants. In capitulating and not pressing my inquiry, I felt more confused than I was before. I didn't feel relieved. I didn't feel satisfied with or appeased by the new information, because there was none. My parents told us nothing. There was something to tell, but they told us nothing.

I stayed up late that night working on the Ababilini diorama. Several times, I got up from my desk and stood outside my parents' bedroom, pressing my back into the wall, listening. I heard a movie playing on TV. I heard them talk about getting the sliding door fixed. When the newspaper shook, I ran back to my room and slid into my seat. For a long time, I eavesdropped on their conversations.

The Four Beloved Things Above came out well, though I encountered some difficulty gluing the yellow fringe around the sun's core such that it didn't droop. For the murderous fisherman, Ben suggested that I create a jug of poison from clay and draw a skull and crossbones on it, boys being proficient at such villainous representations. The man turned out to be pretty petrifying, and his fish, pretty dead indeed, held high into the turquoise sky.

By the end of the night, I truly did hate the Chickasaws and their presumptuous Ababilini and looked forward to explaining why when I returned to school the following morning, the diorama clutched under my arm.

Sixteen

We were to metamorphose from rows to "tables," each consisting of six desks pushed together into a rectangle. Mrs. Colson stood in the center of the classroom with an index card and told us where to go. Each kid stood up, turned his chair upside down on his desk and pushed his pile of furniture to the appointed spot. Changing The Desk Day happened each month. Changing The Desk Day was transformational.

Everybody went where he was supposed to go, even if he wasn't thrilled with his new locale. Contentment was derived from the notion of a new perspective, a fresh slant on third grade. But not for Todd Forrester. When it was his turn, in this final reconfiguration of the year, he did not go where he was supposed to go. He was not interested in a fresh slant. Instead, he had something to say. "I will not sit at Table Three. I will only sit next to Kate. Only!"

Sweet Jesus. I ceased to breathe in my new seat at Table Six.

Mrs. Colson took a step toward him. "Todd, I realize that you'd like to sit next to Kate, but you are going to have to move to Table Three."

He bounced in his Keds. "I have to sit next to her. I have to."

The laughter crescendoed. Mrs. Colson was lost, rendered useless. She put her hand to her forehead, then to her mouth. She flapped the index cards on her hip.

I lifted the top of my desk as far as it would go, to the full seventy degrees, and hid behind the shield that it had become. The pencils spilled out of the pencil depression in the wood and rolled onto the floor. Following them, my body crumpled and crawled underneath.

Girls were not allowed to wear pants or shorts to school in 1969, and we knew how to maneuver our legs so that our underwear remained beneath our skirts and out of public view. I swiveled into position and waited. This was unlike any display I had heard about before, let alone been its target. It seemed like a good idea to stay on the floor.

Mrs. Colson again directed Todd to go to Table Three.

"I can't do that," he said.

The words rang in the metal over my head. Five sets of legs hung around me, like jail bars. I had turned myself in, I suppose, guilty, but of what?

"Well, then, how about if you sit at the same table as Kate, but not next to her?" Mrs. Colson said.

What? A compromise? You don't compromise with anarchists.

Todd rejected the offer. Adjacent or nothing. Overcome by his persistence, Mrs. Colson buckled, selling my equanimity for a restored classroom, like cash for a hostage.

I heard Todd gather up his notebooks and pencils and rulers, cracking them against the formica. I watched his feet plod across the tile. He wore red socks with the double stripe at the cuff, navy and white. His pants, medium stone chinos, were cuffed and very nice, I must admit. As he approached the desk contiguous to mine, I shifted to my knees and dropped my head into my lap. I will have to stay under here for the rest of my life, I thought. I will need a flashlight.

"Where is Kate, anyway?" my friend Julie asked.

"Well, that's a good question," answered Mrs. Colson. Feeble Mrs. Colson. Traitorous Mrs. Colson.

"She's under her desk," said Debbie Thornton.

Thank you, Debbie Thornton. With the disclosure, twenty-four heads flipped upside down. I took a breath and peeked through the fingers covering my face. Julie held onto her glasses so they wouldn't fall off.

Debbie pointed. "Look!"

Todd's crew socks sat at the desk next to mine. He did not turn upside down; such arrogance.

Mrs. Colson squatted to my height, angling her thighs sideways.

"There you are, dear. Why don't you come out and join the class?"

She had to have been psychotic.

"Why won't you come out?" she repeated, inserting her arm through the legs of my desk, as if to snatch me like a gerbil from a cage. Her hand swiveled at the wrist, searching, and I thought to yank it and twist, hard, maiming Mrs. Colson in a wretched and violent way.

Well, Mrs. Colson, since you asked, how about because I have been humiliated by a boy and you and a roomful of kids who are supposed to be my friends. How about that? How about because I am only nine, and I have no idea what I am supposed to do about this and you are not helping. How about that, I screamed, silently, saying nothing.

Changing The Desk Day happened at the end of the day. I had two-fifty-eight on my red Timex. I could endure for seventeen more minutes.

"She's going to let her stay under there," I heard Julie say.

The others bobbed up and down, looking, slapping hands on their desks overhead, shoving their chairs back on the floor. The metal above me reverberated.

In a swoop, all of my classmates became idiots. It was not a rigorous leap, to imagine what I must have felt like, but none of them were able to do it. Lawrence Gardner was the smartest kid in the class. He knew the planets, cold. And the mountain ranges, even the ones in Asia, the obscure Asia, not China and Japan. But Lawrence became an idiot at that moment, too. He could have stood up and told Todd Forrester to be done with his bravado and Mrs. Colson to act like a respectable teacher of young minds. And, in my version of an ideal classroom experience, he could have climbed onto the top of Mrs. Colson's desk, kicked her stupid kangaroo stapler to the linoleum and shamed the rest of the kids into laying off. But Lawrence Gardner did no such things. He sat silently at his desk, in his old location, waiting like a lemming to be told where to go.

Mrs. Colson stretched her knees straight and made her way to the front of the room, her gum soles squeaking like crickets. Heels looked dumb in rubber. She finished making her seating assignments. When Billy Sloate was asked to move to Table One, he jumped up and yelled, "I will not! I will only sit next to Kate!" The crowd roared.

I stayed in hiding while everybody got their book bags from the closet and lined up to leave. Mrs. Colson had the sense to summon the teacher from next door to take the class outside. Once the last of them was gone, she sat down on my vacant chair. Too wide for the seat, her hips bulged over the edge, like water balloons.

"Everybody's outside," she said.

I crept between the legs of the desk and emerged, whacking my ponytail on the way up. I walked to the closet to get my sweater and briefcase, into which I put my work for the next day, my Empire State Building change purse and my spiral assignment pad.

"Do you need help?" Mrs. Colson asked.

"I can do it."

When I was ready, we left the room and headed down the hall. My knees were patched grey.

"It's hard, sometimes." She hugged me around my arms, which hung straight at my sides. My nose mashed into her stomach. "Have a nice walk home."

I got to the sidewalk, somehow, without realizing. My briefcase slapped my hip, and I tried to keep it from bouncing, but my skirt got tucked under and I panicked that my underwear was exposed to the walkers behind me. I tugged it down and a button popped.

"Did you change seats today?" my mother asked when I got home.

I nodded. "Table Three."

"Wow, tables. That's a fun arrangement."

I took off my skirt and handed her the button. She took out a needle and thread from her sewing basket.

Typically, I told my parents about most things that happened to me, in excruciating detail. I generally mentioned the good things, choosing not to convey unpleasant news unless I absolutely had to. I did not tell them about the aquatics counselor who put me in the corner of the pool when I wouldn't open my eyes under the water.

Bad swimmer. I did not tell them when I had felt sick in the back seat of the car and was about to throw up.

"Just say something if you feel queasy," my father would say, every time, after swerving off the road into the grass. After Ben, next to me on the bench seat, would writhe in disgust and Mom would whip around and lurch over the headrest, clutching tissues.

"Okay, I will," I'd say, knowing I wouldn't and lifting up my feet to avoid the mess swishing beneath them.

It would make sense that I'd skip over the Todd Forrester fiasco. But, given that it occurred when it did, after the ruckus at home, I just didn't have the fortitude to manage it privately. And, something about it felt different from the other routine unpleasantries, something momentous, even, about human beings and my place among them. What I didn't know until Changing The Desk Day was that human boys were going to inject themselves into the lives of human girls, whether we wanted them to or not. Sure, I knew that they existed, on Earth, but I didn't know that we would have to deal with them personally, actually respond to them more than you would a can of string beans, for instance. I didn't know that their attention would make me feel cut open and laid out, exposed and suppressed, all at once.

"When we changed the seats, Todd Forrester yelled to everybody that he had to sit next to me and he wouldn't sit anywhere else. And Mrs. Colson let him. So, I went under the desk and stayed there, and that's why I'm dirty."

She stopped sewing and put her hand on my knee. "You know, boys do all kinds of things when they like you."

This was not the kind of comfort I was looking for. I wanted her to say that it wouldn't happen again, the way chicken pox wouldn't happen again. A future of irrational male people unable to restrain themselves, a destiny spent holed up behind partitions and under camelback sofas. I'd be ninety and jogging down the sidewalk with my cane, in a mad escape from some ranting old boy. "Kate Nichols, I will die without you," he'd wail, half-dead already.

My mother finished sewing the button, and I stood up from the couch to go upstairs. She bit off the thread and tossed the skirt to me by the door.

"Made it extra strong," she said. "Like you."

In my bedroom, I sat down at my desk to start my homework, opening the drawer to get a pencil. Instead, I took out a pair of scissors. School had become a refuge from home. I had started to feel less agitated there. I didn't feel powerless or gullible. I was good at taking spelling tests and writing book reports and playing with my friends at recess. But the embarrassment of the day, the callousness of the classmates I believed to be my compatriots, sullied the place. Wherever I turned, there was a minefield.

I threaded my fingers into the scissors, opened it wide and cut up the skirt, sweeping its shreds into the Halloween-pumpkin candy basket stashed under my bed.

That night, I couldn't fall asleep. I rolled around and kicked off the covers. I curled into a kidney bean, walked my feet up the wall, stripped bare. Resigned, I stood and crossed the room, opening the shades. The backyard hill was dark and still, the tree line at the top lit by the moon. An EKG.

I took a small notebook and pens from my desk and sat in the middle of the floor. My naked skin folded on itself and stung, stuck to the tile. I drew in my knees and balanced the pad. On the first page, I wrote: *Things I'm Going to Do When I Grow Up.*

On the second, I started a list.

1. *Not sit near boys, ever, except for Ben*
2. *Do a double pirouette, no, a triple!*
3. *Not keep quiet when I don't want to just because Mom and Dad said to*
4. *Find out about the baby and other stuff, too*

I slid the notebook into my underwear drawer and got back into bed. The sheets felt cool and crisp on my skin. I counted Papa Sam's smoke rings and fell asleep.

SEVENTEEN

PAPA SAM STUFFED FOUR Wiffle balls into one pocket of his bomber jacket. Sucking candies occupied the other, an expansive selection that included butterscotch and root beer as well as the fruits, dotted with Grandma Lilly's sugar-free half-moons. Without much provocation, Papa Sam would pull open the jacket fabric and smile, an invitation for Ben and me to descend upon him like moths and slide our hands in, closing eyes to the sky and extracting a surprise.

He had prepared an activity for our visit the following Sunday, a welcome outing given the teasing I endured the rest of the week at school. When I arrived the day after Todd's announcement, I moved my desk out of the table formation, turning the remaining five into a "C." I pushed it to the side of the class, its feet screeching over the tile, the chair rattling on top. Mrs. Colson called to me, saying something I couldn't hear over the noise. I felt her follow me as I headed for the windows, where I parked the desk. She leaned toward me and said I'd be blocking the bookcase below the sill, pointing to the shelves with her flappy arms, unaware that the prior day's events were enough, that I hid in the bathtub that morning while my parents banged on the door, yelling at me to come out. But before she could suggest an alternative location, I shoved the tower of furniture across the linoleum a second time, nearly to the front of the room, under the flag. No one walked under the flag.

Todd Forrester, of course, initiated a protest, stomping and pointing at me, but Mrs. Colson, showing uncharacteristic leadership, swiftly directed him into the corridor and turned him to face the wall. When she allowed him back inside, he went the long way around to his desk in the "C," ringing the room and passing mine, which he slapped hard as he strode by, baring his teeth. I kept my desk under the flag for the remainder of the school year, unattached to any other grouping, a self-imposed exile. *With liberty and justice for all.*

The golf clubs were waiting by the door when we arrived in Belle Harbor. Papa Sam put on his cap and grabbed them.

"Kate's going to have a little instruction, and then we'll go to the range," he told Ben.

My golf club was a miniature version of his, a real steel putter with a tan leather grip. We went around the house and through the gate to the small yard. Newly planted petunias circled the perimeter, anchored with hydrangea bushes in the corners, set to bloom violet and pink. If you dig a hole and put a penny into the soil, Grandma Lilly said, the flowers grow extra petals. Papa Sam took the balls from his pocket and draped his jacket over an Adirondack chair, which Grandma Lilly had painted blue. A cornflower, verging on azure.

"Look at that sky," he said. "A perfect day."

He walked onto the grass and inserted a wooden tee into the lawn, and with the same magical motion that produced coins from my ear or shadow rabbits and monkeys on my wall, a ball materialized in the ethers and perched atop the peg. He showed me how to grasp the grip, locking his right pinkie over his left thumb, opening and closing his palms to demonstrate.

Agile and manicured, his hands were his livelihood, and as my father did, Papa Sam took care of them. He didn't do heavy work or fix cars. He wore gloves at the hint of a chill. To protect the fabrics from nicking and snags, he kept his nails short and filed and skin smooth.

He turned me toward the tee. "Now put your feet here and here, like one of your ballet positions."

"It's second, except for the toes." I angled them out and then back in. "Like this."

"Good, now bend your knees…just a little."

"Demi-plie!"

"Demi-plie."

Keeping my arms straight, I drew the club back and swung, sending the ball through the grass. Papa Sam placed the remaining three balls on the tee, and I hit each one in succession.

"You are quite the golfer," he said. "And quite the big girl."

"I'm only nine."

"But you're learning all kinds of things. Important things."

I supposed he was talking about my running away and everything that came after it, checking to see how I was holding up. I figured he would at some point in our visit, even though we had already spoken about it on the phone. I didn't know if Mom ever told him that I knew about his baby, and I had no idea if he was aware of my parents' secret. It was a lot to keep straight.

"Your family means everything, and you have to take care of it, right?"

I could have asked him at that moment, about his family, about how he tried to take care of it. I didn't know what he was saying, really. There was a crinkle in his brow, a hint of sorrow, and I felt sad for him. I felt the weight of his loss and now, having been reminded of the impact of my own actions, the responsibility.

"Right, Papa."

He placed an empty can of beets on its side at the end of the grass. "Now aim."

I lined up my feet in front of the tee. "I'm sorry...about running away and scaring you. About everything."

He wrapped his hands around mine and wiggled my grip. "I know, and don't worry. You're safe, so we're all okay."

The six of us got into the Oldsmobile and headed for the driving range. I sat in back with my parents, and Ben slid into the middle seat in front. He got to work the radio. I reached forward to tickle the back of his neck, but Dad tapped my arm.

"He could bump into the driver. Never disturb the driver."

In the operating room, my father had seen the consequences of bad choices. A loose shoelace on an escalator? Lose your foot, or worse. A hair dryer on the bathroom vanity? Electrocution.

Grandma Lilly's was the highest of the three heads, what with her Friday afternoon salon visits. She wore her hair tall and teased, with two symmetrical waves above the center of her forehead, a Victorian scroll. It was a formal hairdo, wanting jewelry and silk dresses, but it remained the same every day, at all hours, no matter the cotton skirt or nightgown beneath it.

"Evie," she said, looking at my mom in the makeup mirror. "Remember how we came here when you were the children's age?"

"I can't believe it's still standing."

"It's a landmark. Everyone comes from all over now."

"I remember carrying the bucket."

"With two arms, it was so heavy."

Papa Sam crunched the Oldsmobile onto the gravel and found a place to park. Beyond the fence, a massive lawn rolled out for acres, if not to Montana. At the concession, Papa Sam picked out clubs for everyone, measuring them against our legs to determine the correct size.

"You've got the whole crew today," said the man behind the counter.

"Wait till you see these two hit the ball."

Dad picked up the two metal buckets of balls and led the way onto the path, where wooden tee platforms had been placed every ten feet, holes in a belt.

"C'mon," Ben said, spotting two next to each other and grabbing my arm. We ran ahead and jumped on top of the artificial grass. "I'm going to hit them way out to those houses."

I looked back and watched my parents and grandparents approach, Mom in a yellow wrap-around skirt, Grandma Lilly looking young and sporty in pale pink Bermudas and espadrilles. Papa Sam had taken one of the buckets from Dad, and the two walked in stride, with dueling grins.

Though Papa Sam had quit college to help support his three siblings, he was a lifelong student who read to learn, marking up margins in pencil. An engineer at heart, he had shelves of books that explained how to make gadgets and gizmos, how to do most any-thing, really. In his car trunk, he kept a prized invention, a tool that could measure the speed of a swing. The ball sat on a metal tee that swiveled when it was struck, counting revolutions and translating them into units of velocity. A training mechanism for self-improve-ment. Papa Sam carried it to the range so we could try it.

He and Dad shared humble beginnings and sweeping curiosity. I inherited a double dose of the latter.

Papa Sam put a ball on each of the tees and stood between the platforms. "Let's see your stances."

We wiggled into position.

"Now, your grips."

We unfolded them for inspection and curled them back in.

"You are ready. Fire away."

We took turns, each of us hitting two balls at a time. When Grandma Lilly stepped onto the platform, we all turned to watch. She set her feet on either side of the tee, adjusting her delicate an-kles, swaying her hips.

Papa Sam rocked forward and back on his toes. "Watch this."

Like an explorer claiming her land, she planted the head of the club on the turf and surveyed the field. "To the left, by the oak trees." She smiled devilishly.

The oaks were far away, and the angle was difficult.

"She'll do it," Papa Sam said quietly. "She has the magic touch."

Grandma Lilly brought the club around to the front of her body and placed it behind the ball, lengthening her arms, like needles. She lowered her chin, and her kerchief caught a breeze, its point shooting up, becoming taut. In one fluid motion, she pulled back the club, swiveled, raised a heel, and brought the head back down upon the ball, lifting it with a crack and sending it exactly where she had intended. I followed the trajectory as the backdrop changed, from grass to sky to tree and grass again. We all clapped, and Grand-ma Lilly spun around toward us and curtsied.

"Now you go, Evie," Papa Sam said, kissing Lilly's cheek.

"After that, don't be expecting much."

"Go ahead, sweetie, just have fun," said Lilly. "And pick a spot. That's the trick."

"How did you learn to hit like that?" Dad asked.

"Two older brothers, and then Sammy. There was no way I wouldn't know how."

As afternoons went, this one was pretty exceptional. I didn't overhear Mom and Dad arguing about anything mysterious. Not for a minute did I believe that Grandma Lilly was thinking about her baby boy. I wasn't compelled to rip something up or run away or throw an object across the driving range lawn, and no nine-year-old boy mortified me with his undying affection. I hoped that maybe, this was a watershed, the moment when bad switched back to good, as much as you can know this at the time, actually recognize the point at which a situation turns. I sensed some kind of peace in the faces and bodies of my family, in the lack of tension in my shoulders, the lightness in my step. I didn't whack the ball; I sent it soaring, freely, like a dove to the heavens.

Papa Sam sat next to me on the bench and lifted open his pocket. I reached in and pulled out a sour cherry, the kind that tingles at the back of your cheeks, that makes your eyes water. That makes them well up and blink so much that you have to say you aren't crying, that it's the candy, that you are just so happy.

PART TWO
1972

EIGHTEEN

MY MOTHER CROSSED THE living room to the piano, where I was practicing after school. "Grandpa Leo died. Did you know that?"

I was twelve. I hadn't received word from the authorities, no. A doctor hadn't called me, or an ambulance driver or a policeman, to say, "Miss Nichols, we've been trying to find you. We did everything that we could." The news hadn't risen from the chords and arpeggios in my hands. I was not telepathic.

Before I could answer her question, if I was even going to answer, she turned around and walked back across the shocking pink carpet and up the steps to throw her school sack and pocketbook and keys and whatever else onto the pile of detritus by my parents' bedroom door. I sat on the piano bench, lightheaded, trembling, my feet dangling. The sudden announcement bludgeoned me. I was paralyzed, unable to move. Should I play? Should I get up? What do you do when someone dies? What do you do when someone dies and your mother leaves you alone with the blow?

I hadn't experienced the death of a person whom I had known and loved. It didn't feel like the loss of the wild bunny or my infant uncle or the soldiers on TV. I was fully conscious for those. This numbed me, put me in some anesthetized state, and it hurt me, too, profoundly and thoroughly. I felt cracked in the face, but I remained upright, the pain dispersing into my neck and torso and limbs.

Some minutes later, my father ascended the stairs, home early from work. In a split-level, you can see the person's head first, and then the rest of him floats from the depths. From the piano bench, I saw his brown hair, light and reddish in the sidelight sun, and then his profile, his arrow-straight nose, well-proportioned chin. Next came his white shirt and suited hips, legs, ankles, wing-tips. He skipped steps, as usual, with pace, turning a right angle at the second flight and disappearing down the hall. He did not look my way. I did not call out or run to him. The bedroom door shut tight. I sat on the bench and closed the cover over the keys. We had become a family that shut doors.

A while later, Angie found me in my bedroom and said it was time for dinner. I had been adding to the Grow Up List since starting it that night in third grade. This day, the notation was obvious: *Not leave someone alone when her grandfather dies and she doesn't know what to do*

Angie took me by the hand to the kitchen, where Ben was waiting. The room felt warm from the oven. "Did you see Dad?"

Ben shook his head. His eyes were puffy.

I turned to Angie. "Can you eat with us?"

She brought three plates of meatloaf and mashed potatoes to the table and put bowls of green beans and salad in front of us. A platter of homemade chocolate cookies waited on the counter, freshly baked.

"Sit here," I said, patting my mother's chair, which was next to mine.

Angie situated herself and extended her arms flat on the table, sliding one toward me, the other toward Ben. We put our hands in hers. She looked at each of us, intently, and said that she felt so sorry that Grandpa Leo had died, and that he knew that we loved him. "It hurts when someone goes, and it makes you feel helpless. Just helpless."

I burst into tears and fell onto her chest. Ben got up and held her from the other side. She grasped us both and started to hum. It was a solemn and soulful sound, and it reverberated through me, into my brain and lungs and belly, making me stop thinking, right there, right then. I had questions, so many questions about what had happened to my grandfather and how he could possibly be gone.

So quickly. So definitively. I hung onto her notes, and her, and we rocked, so slightly, even after her singing was done.

———————

Not sure whether my parents would come down to eat, Angie wrapped the food, and we helped her put it in the fridge and clear the dishes. Usually, she would end her day at this point, retiring to the finished basement, a large rectangle with a trapezoidal alcove cut into one of the walls, long enough for a twin bed, wide enough for a chest of drawers. My mother had provided bolsters for the bed, so it could pretend to be a couch during the daytime. I liked sitting in her room after school sometimes, perfume spray bottles in line on a tray, library novels stacked. Sometimes, we played word games in a spiral notebook. She kept the light on only in the alcove. You knew the basement lay beyond, but you couldn't see it.

This night, Angie stayed with us, accompanying us back to our rooms to carry out the evening routine, as much as there could be one after the day's events. My parents' door remained closed, and I couldn't hear any words being spoken, not even a murmur. We went into the hallway, and I stood for a minute by their room. It had been several hours since we had seen them. I didn't know what we were supposed to do.

Angie watched.

Ben shook his head and whispered. "Don't go in. Don't."

He didn't realize that since overhearing our parents in the kitchen two and a half years earlier, I had stationed myself outside their bedroom many times, eavesdropping on their conversations. The practice had become routine, and it extended beyond the upstairs hallway. When they sat on the back patio, I opened my window and cupped my ear to the screen. I even snooped in plain sight, riding my bike when they took a walk, disappearing and returning without warning, swooping around them in figure eights. I never heard any specifics about what I believed to be a pact, but I thought they referred to it, and me.

In the weeks after I ran away, my father's voice rose up from the picnic table. "If we don't tell her, that's fine."

I also found out that someone stole money from Mr. Brant at his job and that one of the lanky Spector boys had curvature of the spine.

"You shouldn't knock," Ben said.

Unlike the secrets, which I both wanted to know about and was afraid to know about, Grandpa Leo's death had a clear explanation. I needed to know what had happened. I needed to see my father. I needed not to feel helpless anymore. I wondered when people finally got to take charge. Was there a time on the clock when you are allowed, when you cross into unprotected territory, or do you decide that for yourself? I put my hand on the knob and turned.

"You'll bother them," Ben said. "They'll tell us when they're ready."

I opened the door and walked inside. Dad sat at a small desk by the window, writing. The tub ran in the bathroom. I walked carefully across the rug, my father's swollen eyes redder with each step. He tilted his head and put down the pen, and I grabbed him around his chest as far as I could reach, clutching his shirt with my fists, hanging on.

––––––––––––––

The next day, I wrote a letter to Nana Sofie and gave it to Dad before he left to see her.

Dear Nana Sofie,

I am very sad about Grandpa Leo and I miss him so much. He was a great grandfather, chef and chess player. I love you and him and I'm sorry this happened and you are by yourself, but we will visit you more now. I'm glad that Dad reminds me of Grandpa Leo.

Love,
your granddaughter,
Kate Nichols

––––––––––––––

Dad said later that day that Grandpa Leo died from a heart attack. A myocardial infarction, one of the leading causes of death in the United States. This happens when the blood flow to the heart muscle has been blocked, and without the oxygen that's in the blood, the heart can't survive. Typically, Dad explained, fat and cholesterol from food build up in the bloodstream and cause the blockage to form.

"Did he eat something and then die?" I asked.

"It happens over a period of time. But sometimes, it's not the patient's diet that causes it."

"What else, then?" asked Ben.

"Well, clots can form from other factors, or smoking or obesity can make a person susceptible."

"Papa Leo didn't smoke, and he wasn't obese. That's fat, right?"

"Right, and he had good eating habits."

"Where was he?" I asked.

Dad tightened his lips, squeezed his own hands. "At home."

"Where?"

Ben pushed on my leg.

"He was repairing the roof."

"How did he get down?"

"Kate, stop," Ben said.

Dad patted Ben's back. "It's okay. He came down the ladder and sat on the couch." Then he stood and left the room.

"Why did you ask that?" Ben said. "Don't ask those things."

———

Ben and I hadn't been to a funeral before. Mom told us that there would be a ceremony in two days, and people would come and sit in the pews behind us. Everyone would wear black. After, we'd go to Aunt Eleanor's house for lunch.

"I don't have anything black," I said. Little girls wore colors in 1972.

"It's fine to wear something dark, then. Maybe the maroon dress?"

I thought of the people in the rows of benches, black suits, black dresses, shoulder to shoulder. I thought of the wall of black and then the maroon, a mistake, calling attention. I may as well have worn magenta polka-dots.

"I want to wear what you're supposed to wear."

My mother stamped a foot. "We just can't go shopping now."

Later, I opened the drawers in the back closet where we kept the fabric. Underneath remnants of plaids and stripes, I found some black cotton and stretched it open. It was textured, with a small paisley design, but it was a solid color. I turned out the light and took it to my mom in the den downstairs. "Can we make a skirt?"

"I really don't think I have the time now, to start sewing clothes. What is wrong with the maroon dress?"

Everything was wrong with the maroon dress. "I'll do it."

"Just don't. Now's not the time."

I thought that now was the perfect time. I went back to the closet and dug through the patterns, finding the one for a simple skirt that we had made before. I laid out the fabric on the floor and tried to smooth out the creases with my hands. When that didn't work, I got a cup of water from the bathroom and wet the lines, figuring that I shouldn't use the iron by myself. The skirt was shirred, which meant that it had only two seams, besides the waist and hem. There would be just a front and back to cut, and I felt confident that I could do it.

On my knees, I maneuvered the pattern pieces to fit them on the fabric and pinned them in place. The trick was to pinch the paper and the cloth at once without causing one to shift. It was difficult to do, and I had to pull out some pins and start over a few times. It must have been an hour before I heard my mother come up the stairs.

"What is this?" she asked, looking down at me.

I continued pinning. "A skirt."

"I said I couldn't do this now."

"You don't have to. I only need you to hold the elastic, to measure it on me, but I can probably do that myself." I sat cross-legged and looked at her. "I can thread the machine."

"I already told you no. I have to deal with your father now, and this is not important. No one cares what you wear to a funeral."

"It's my grandfather's funeral."

She peered down at me. The skin around her mouth fell forward. "You need to listen better."

My mother didn't feel bad for Leo. I understood in that moment that he was my family, but he wasn't hers. Families have dividing lines, boundaries between allegiances, like fractures in bone. "Why don't you like them? Any of them?"

"You'll have in-laws one day, you'll see."

She turned and walked down the hall, throwing up her hands.

———————

We got up early the morning of the service. I couldn't sleep well the night before, nervous about seeing a casket, about being in a room with a dead person. It couldn't be Grandpa Leo in the coffin. Grandpa Leo never took a rest, never stopped working or reading or cooking. It was now some dead person in the box, someone else, someone foreign and scary. In movies, I had seen people collapse on top of the caskets, wailing and clawing for the person inside. It didn't feel to me that Grandpa Leo was inside. He was still at home in his yellow house with the porch in front.

The skirt came out nicely, even the hem, which I sewed by hand. Mom turned up everything with needle and thread, even our dungarees. I had learned well. I shirred the fabric a little extra, so it was full, like a long tutu. I put it on, with a white shirt like my father's and Ben's, black tights and patent leather party shoes. Grandpa Leo said that I looked like a Russian actress when my hair was in a headband, so I wore a black velvet one with a bow on the side.

"You look very pretty," Dad said. "It's a lovely thing that you made the skirt."

We drove somewhere I hadn't been before, taking the same highway we always took but then veering off. It was a windy day, and I cracked the window to hear the whistle and whoosh. Ben and I didn't say much in the car. Mom put her hand on the back of Dad's shoulder. I hoped that I didn't have to sit next to her at the ceremony.

Inside the building, a man in a silver tie led us to a room with flowered couches and a marble coffee table and showed us where to hang our coats on a rack. After a few minutes, the door opened, and Nana Sofie entered, stepping slowly, with Aunt Eleanor and Uncle Roger at her side. Our cousins, ten and twelve years older than I was, followed behind.

I didn't know whether I could go to my grandmother and hug her, or talk to her, or what about. I sensed that this was a situation, this entire dying and funeral-making situation, that was predicated upon rules and procedures, most of which I hadn't learned. There were the straightforward ones—the dressing in black, the fancy room for greeting the family. But there were others that were less obvious, that dictated protection of people's states of mind, fears and apprehensions. Take sweets to the family to ease their burden. Sit at home with them for seven days to give them chairs and snacks and napkins to prepare, chores to do. Write an epitaph a year later and meet again to lay it in the ground.

Standing in the fancy room, I thought about Grandma Lilly. She had no benefit of such rules when her baby died. She had no rituals that would try to distract her or assist her or help handle her grief. She had no people in black clothing, filling in rows behind her, holding her up.

I stood across the room and watched my father take his mother's arm and guide her to the couch. She had put on nicer shoes, not the wide and clunky ones that helped her walk. I stood across the room and watched my aunt dry her eyes with a handkerchief, one of Grandpa Leo's. It was a dance, this caring that we human beings know to do, that we step into like a glissade, a traveling motion from one feeling to the next. It is better choreographed in certain people than in others, and I was realizing that I was among them.

Nana Sofie looked at me and lifted her hand. I sat next to her on the flowered sofa, and she stroked my face, whimpering. "You wrote words that I will treasure forever."

She looked into my eyes, helpless, begging for this not to be, for relief. I stared back at her, feeling her hand on my cheek, feeling her fingers circle on my skin, up and around. Up and around.

NINETEEN

MENSTRUATION DID NOT COMMENCE the day I turned thirteen or even earlier, despite my parents' predictions. And I wasn't concerned about its imminent arrival. After Mr. Milanesi's discovery under my shorts and the subsequent pad-wearing, which I kept up for some weeks despite my mother's intervention, I conducted my own independent research in the World Book Encyclopedia, Book M. It was only then that I stopped wearing the pads to school, convinced that I indeed had some time. A year later, fifth-grade health class solidified the knowledge, and when my friends began the indoctrination into womanhood, it was all anybody talked about at school. My mother was still sort of awkward about it, even when I told her that the menstrual cycle was no big deal, just a normal shedding of the uterine lining. The science diffused my fear, and I embraced the blood, in all its wonder. I came to think that the whole process was pretty spectacular.

To celebrate my teenhood, incomplete as it was without the bleeding, Mom held a boy-girl party in our basement, a birthday surprise at which she instructed my friend Nanette to initiate a game of Spin the Bottle. Nanette was larger than life, what with a five-seven frame and bras, actual bras.

"It's at the top of the stairs," Mom whispered to her, thinking I didn't hear. "The soda bottle. Look."

That my mother conceived, planned and executed the party was a humiliating reality all by itself, without the kissing game. I knew the kids who were in my basement, but it felt weird having them there. I would have felt peculiar in their basements, too. It wasn't that I lacked friends. We just didn't spend much time together outside of school. All day on Saturdays, I took ballet class in Manhattan, so by the time I got home, I just watched TV with my parents or Ben, if they were around. On some Friday nights, I went to a friend's house but had to get to sleep early for the drive into the city.

For the party, my mother had decorated the room to look like a discotheque. A beaded curtain walled off Angie's trapezoid. Pink and blue light bulbs had replaced the regular ones. Sparkly silver balls hung down from the ceiling. On Saturdays, Angie went home to Brooklyn, so the room was available for the pre-pubescent socializing that Mom had concocted for me.

At the bottom of the steps, selected classmates huddled in a singular undulating mound, like kittens in a sack.

"Surprise!" it yelled.

"Turn around, Katie," Dad said from the staircase, having slipped in without notice, camera poised.

Mom squeezed my waist and scrunched in close. Big kiss. Snap, snap.

I surveyed the room. It appeared that there were about twenty-two kids in my basement, among them, to both my horror and unbridled delight, Charlie Rogers, a boy who made me nervous and giddy and uncomfortable and electrified, all at once. A boy who tripped up my toes and tangled my thoughts, who commanded my imaginings of love and romance, nascent though they were, a boy who had walked into Social Studies one Tuesday and reset time and experience. Charlie Rogers was my personal Anno Domini.

Of course, no one in the basement, or anywhere on either hemisphere of the globe, knew that I had been engaging in a private effort to keep his effects on me under wraps. So, whoever made the guest list for my mother had no idea to leave him off of it, unaware that his presence on my street, let alone in my foyer, on my staircase, in the ethers where I existed in my purest and rawest form, would render me unable to form intelligible sentences or breathe without the aid of medical support. And, having confided in only Fifi and Gigi, whose advice was mixed and a bit obsolete, I was on my own.

For the first part of the party, I maneuvered around the edges, keeping a buffer of bodies between Charlie and me, including that of Todd Forrester, who, in the four years since Changing the Desk Day hadn't become any less intrusive. He was actually a competent blockade, a useful annoyance in such a predicament. The distance that I kept from Charlie and the decision not to look at him—too much—helped moderate the breathing in my chest. I knew how to take my pulse, and though slightly elevated, it was within an acceptable range. I feared, though, that Nanette would actually go through with my mother's kissing agenda, at which point Charlie would be in full view, exuding maximum potency in my unprotected direction.

Sure enough, Nanette grabbed the bottle and instructed my guests to form a circle on the floor. They slid into place, appearing to have played the game before. I, of course, hadn't, and was mortified that it would be foisted upon me for the first time in my discotheque basement, at my mother's suggestion. Clearly, I lagged, experientially, but I was curious, and I was newly teened. I had the hormones, whether I was ready for them or not. Despite my flourishing endocrine system, there was no way that I could sit in the circle forming mere feet from Angie's bedroom, the premise for which was to touch, let alone kiss, the anatomy of the boys in my class.

I slipped out of the room and up the two flights to the living room, where my parents were eating turkey sandwiches. Ben was at a school function.

My mother looked up from her plate. "Having fun?"

"Spin the Bottle? How could you do this to me?"

Dad crunched on a potato chip. "What is she talking about?"

"She put a bottle down there to spin around and kiss people. How could you expect me to do that? I haven't ever kissed a boy, and I don't want to. Anywhere. Especially not in my basement in front of my entire class."

"You did that, Eva? Some of these kids are only twelve."

"She gave it to Nanette. I can't believe this."

My mother took a sip of ginger ale. "We all played when we were

112

that age, it's no big deal."

"You? What? I don't do these things. Me, Kate. Not you."

"It wouldn't hurt you to have a little fun. You're too serious, like your father. Two peas."

"This isn't fun. It's the opposite of fun. Dad, please do something. I can't go back down there."

"You do not have to play, but you'll have to go downstairs at some point, since it's your party."

"And you could have asked me if I wanted a stupid party. No mothers throw parties anymore."

Dad gave my mother a knowing look. "Maybe in a few minutes, you can go collect some cups and plates, make yourself busy being a hostess, without joining in."

"And say what when they ask me?"

"Say you're going to sit this one out and suggest another activity. Eva, give her an orange for that passing game."

"Oh god, that will never work. This is horrifying."

I grabbed a trash bag from the kitchen and approached the staircase. Halfway down, I could see Richie Stillman, spinning. As the bottle rotated, everyone in the circle shook and squealed. The boys who weren't Charlie Rogers fell over onto the linoleum, making raucous, guttural sounds. The girls, sitting cross-legged, bobbed their knees up and down.

Lauren Dempsey saw me enter the room and waved me over, making room next to her. No one else paid much attention.

"I have to clean up a little. Give me a minute."

Richie Stillman had given the bottle a robust twist. When the spinning slowed, the Oooooooh began, ratcheting into shrieks as the bottle stopped turning and pointed at the kissee. Without hesitation, Richie crawled across the circle and while still on his knees, kissed Jenny Mills, who had thrown her palms to her forehead, squeezed her eyes shut and presented her cheek.

I collected stray cups and plates and dropped them into the garbage bag, watching the action from the far side of the basement. It looked harmless; Jenny Mills had survived, and she wasn't a wild kid either. I didn't know how she did it. Some part of me wanted to sit in the circle, to do what other kids did comfortably. But that night, I was so mad, and I wanted to hide, and I wanted everyone to hurry up and go home.

Without my noticing, Nanette appeared next to me, took the bag and set it down in the corner. "It's your birthday, you have to play. C'mon."

"It's okay, I'm just going to clean up."

"If it lands on you, just turn your cheek. A lot of kids do that."

"Really?"

"Yeah, they do. I've done it."

She led me to the circle and tapped the floor next to her. Charlie sat at one o'clock. I was at eight, fortunately, as far from him as possible without sharing the diameter. I looked everywhere but at him, his twinkly eyes, his messy blond hair, his hands, neat and lithe despite his age. My ventricles went haywire. I thought my aorta would burst.

Nanette gave the bottle to Susie Ross, her best friend. Susie Ross was self-assured and pretty. She skied in the winter with her older brothers, high school soccer players with scoring records and photos in the local paper. They were Norsemen of the Week, nearly every week. Susie played the guitar and sang Joni Mitchell songs. She stood and gave the bottle a solid flip, swaying her hips in the center of the circle as it turned, shaking her shagged hair over her face. In our refrigerator just days earlier, filled with root beer, the bottle was now out of place, a hostage, too. It wobbled as it spun, slowing… eleven o'clock, twelve, one. The neck pointed to Charlie. Charlie Rogers. That Charlie Rogers.

Immediately, the boys swatted his blond locks and grabbed his well-proportioned shoulders. They blurted his name and whistled. Perspiration soaked my underarms. Susie Ross stood in the circle, waiting, one confident hand on her hip. Charlie hopped up, shook out his dungarees and looked away, gathering courage. I hoped in that moment of hesitation that he would sit back down on my basement floor, realizing that he couldn't kiss Susie Ross, not in front of me, anyway, the girl he really liked but hadn't yet told, the girl who sat across the circle at eight o'clock, melting into oblivion, steaming with jealousy, that girl. But he swiveled back around and walked slowly to her, head down, tilted a smidge, smiling in that demure way that only he smiled, the way I wanted him to smile at me, the way that I hallucinated about three rows over in Social Studies. When he faced her, he raised his chin and pecked her on the cheek, polite and chivalrous as I knew he was, without knowing him at all, without ever having a conversation of more than sixteen words, maybe about turning in homework or the Early Roman Empire. Not to be given short shrift, Susie Ross put her other hand on her other hip and tapped her wedge-heeled foot, signaling to the crowd, if not to Charlie, that his peck would not do. No, lips or nothing. I thought I'd hyperventilate and die.

Head between my knees, I didn't notice when Todd Forrester twirled the bottle next, and it landed on me. Hearing my name sail through the air, cackling like a pileated woodpecker, I straightened my neck and saw my future, as well as my past. Todd Forrester's chinoed knees, planted firmly in front of my face, demanding, expectant, horrifying. I ricocheted back to Mrs. Colson's third-grade classroom, trapped under the desks, a victim of unwanted public affection.

The discotheque basement thumped. Kids hollered in disbelief. Boys tackled Todd, celebrating his luck, catapulting in a pile of limbs in front of me. Todd got to his knees, and the boys pushed him toward me. I slid backward but they kept pushing, his teeth, his tongue, his lips inflating as he approached. I squeezed my eyes shut like Jenny Mills and clenched my hands over my mouth.

"Do it already," I yelled through my fist.

In seconds, his face smacked into mine, and I felt his lips purse into a hard ball and then come apart, like the huge koi fish in Miss Kellerman's pond. Revolted, I slung off his slobber with my sleeve and ran up the stairs to the bathroom sink, sending my assembled birthday guests into a frenzy, lighting the hormonal swell with kindling. My entire face doused and dripping, I headed for my bedroom, finding a different sweater laid out on my bed, the one adorned with a pink and gold sequinned ice cream cone. Mom had thought that I should wear this to the surprise birthday party instead of what I already had on. She believed I would want to go upstairs and change my clothes and return to the basement, exhilarated, ready to kiss boys I hardly said hello to in the junior high hallway. Ready to manage my emotions when I couldn't. To be someone who was not me.

Strains of "Penny Lane" sailed through the air conditioning vent, under fits of pandemonium. I did not return to the discotheque basement or to the front door when everyone left, even though my parents said I was being rude.

The next Monday, Todd Forrester broadcast to the entire school population that he had kissed me and that I had let him.

TWENTY

SOON AFTER THE DISCOTHEQUE birthday, Papa Sam determined that Lill-Dor Fashions Inc. had run its course. When the company was in full swing in the 1950s, he said that racks of dresses tore through New York City's streets on the West side like cars, traveling from the factories to the stores. But soon after I was born, he had to move his workroom upstate to Kingston, where he could pay less for rent. Before dawn each Wednesday, he drove a hundred miles north, arriving in time for a full day at the factory. He stayed overnight in a hotel and after work on Thursday, he returned to Belle Harbor. He spent the other three days of the week at the Manhattan show-room, where his partner handled operations in his absence. It was a rigorous schedule, but Papa Sam loved the work, even after so many decades in the business.

He had convinced Lilly to move to Florida, where they could continue to live near the ocean, without the snow and frost. And us. We saw them less, now that Ben and I were getting older and more involved with school and activities, but we still spent time with them at regular intervals and on family occasions. I was surprised when they told us they were leaving, though I understood that Papa Sam was eager for the change, for what must have promised to be an ongoing vacation after so many years of hard work. I wasn't sure that Grandma Lilly viewed the adventure with similar enthusiasm.

A week before they were to go, we visited them in Belle Harbor. It would be our last drive to Neptune Avenue, into the water tow-er tank and out, up the staircase of the navy-and-white house. We wouldn't go to the beach there anymore. There was one closer, if we even were to go. Our town had a pool.

Grandma Lilly tilted her head toward the bedroom. "Come with me."

Suitcases were packed and standing in the corner. A round ivory one lay flat on top. "It's a hat box," she said. "No one uses them anymore. Go ahead, you can open it."

Inside, the case was lined with a stiff violet satin, textured like grosgrain ribbon. A stack of hats filled the diameter, the widest brims at the bottom, tapering off to the top. There were huge straw ones for the sun, slim cartwheels and prim boaters. For fall, felt cloches, berets, and a patent leather derby I remembered from a Thanksgiving downpour. I picked up a baby blue turban from the top of the pile and spun it in my hand.

"It goes like this." Grandma Lilly plunked it on her head and nudged it into place. "We wore these in the 40s, sometimes with a big rhinestone pin…very glamorous." She took it off and stretched it over my ponytails.

I would miss hearing about my grandparents' lives and seeing the objects that told their stories.

"I have something for you," she said.

From the top drawer of the dresser, she took out a small gray box and handed it to me. I set it down and opened the cover.

"For special occasions," she said.

Under a puff of cotton, I found a gold locket on a chain, an oval carved with a minuscule bouquet of flowers in its center. I lifted the necklace out of the box and held it to the light. "Does it open?"

She nodded.

Inside, there were two photographs, one of her and one of Papa Sam. Quickly, I took the ends of the chain and tried to clasp them behind my neck. Grandma Lilly stepped behind me and secured the latch, turning my shoulders toward the mirror and holding on. The locket landed in the perfect spot, right where the collar bones meet. I felt the first burn of tears. We stood smiling at each other in the glass, a portrait, my grandmother's polished pink nails grounding me, her baby blue turban corralling my thoughts.

"Do you have to go?"

"I think so. But you'll come on vacation. We're going to have a big room for you."

"It's going to be different. Do you think you'll like it?"

She pressed her cheek against mine, and I felt her hairdo through the turban. "I have no idea, but I hope."

TWENTY-ONE

MOM SENT FLORAL QUILTS the first week they were gone. Nothing helps to ground a transition like bedding. Then, she went on a hunt for a mah-jongg set. Grandma Lilly didn't play games with other women in Belle Harbor, but she mentioned that a lot of people in Florida socialized this way, and she decided to give it a try. Mom made calls to stores around the county and found an unusually beautiful set with blush pink tiles. Every other day, it seemed she went to the post office to mail something to Grandma Lilly—soaps, stationery, perfume.

Papa Sam quickly acclimated to the southern lifestyle. He got up early and walked along the beach promenade. He joined the apartment building's shuffleboard team, never having played but reading ahead of time about proper form and winning strategies. His teammates appointed him Captain within weeks. Soon, he had joined the Board of the building, attending meetings about lobby upholstery, elevator maintenance and other such concerns of condominium living. He befriended all comers.

I was used to seeing them once or twice a month, and I felt a defined change once they were gone. Previously, my grandparents could be present whenever we all chose. After the move, the new expectation felt limiting. I feared that I had likely learned all that I would from them, that I had known them as well as I ever would, that our relationship was, in a way, finished. For me, their leaving was premature, and it felt final.

We visited for the first time during our Christmas vacation, about five months after the move. I was not yet fourteen.

"Look at that sky," Papa Sam said, even when clouds threatened to drizzle. "It's quite a day."

I learned how to push the puck down the shuffleboard court, lifting a leg behind me as Papa Sam did. Dad planned excursions to historical museums, Spanish gardens and marine habitats. I sat at the pool with Grandma Lilly, meeting her neighbors and talking about ballet and boys, whom she introduced as an acceptable topic, now that I was a viable adolescent. She said I didn't have to like them until I was ready, and that would likely come soon. She didn't know about Charlie Rogers. Mostly, she talked, and I listened.

We returned home to New York rested and tired all at once, sunburn prickly under our winter sweaters, reassured that all was well in the Goldman household.

When I was fifteen, Grandma Lilly began calling more often. One day, I saw Mom on the kitchen phone, looking concerned.

"What is it?" I motioned.

She covered up the receiver. "Grandma is acting a little funny."

"What do you mean?"

"That's not true," she said into the phone. "Mom? Are you there?" She shook her head and redialed. "No, you're not dying. Your doctors say you are a picture of health."

She covered up the receiver again. "She's fine, don't worry. She just says this."

People didn't just say this. "We have to do something," I said after Mom finished the call. "She could be sick. You can't just hang up when she says that."

"She'll be fine."

"You don't know that."

"It's emotional, maybe a change of life."

"What?"

"Women go through phases."

I waited.

"First they have babies, then they can't have them anymore, and then they get older and everyone goes away and they miss being younger. It's rough."

"Okay, but dying? What did Dad say?"

"He said she needs a psychiatrist."

"And Papa Sam? Not that he ever thinks anything isn't perfect."

"He said she's just out of sorts sometimes. And that they've been to some parties lately and she loves the mah-jongg ladies."

"Can we go over mid-winter vacation?"

"We weren't planning on it. It's a lot to arrange, and we can't just go run there every time there's something."

It wasn't that Grandma Lilly lacked friends or hated the weather or simply missed her home. Those problems wouldn't cause you to think you were going to die and tell your daughter about your imminent demise in hushed tones, from thirteen hundred miles away. My parents had so many responsibilities that one could get in the way of another. I understood all about priorities—schoolwork first, dance second—but this felt to me that it should be higher on the list.

Meantime, I would do my own investigating. A few days later, I called Grandma Lilly.

Papa Sam answered. "She'll be thrilled to hear from you. Hold on, she's right here."

It took longer than it should have.

"Just a second, I'm sitting up," she said, faintly. I looked at my watch. Three o'clock. "How are you, and Ben? It's so nice you called."

"We are good. What about you? How is the mah-jongg?"

"Ah, those women. Not for me." Her voice was frail.

"Why not?"

"They're snooty."

"All of them?"

"Sally's nice," Papa Sam said in the background.

"Oh, hush. She has a poodle who's nice, but that's it. Gray, with little white feet. Sits on her lap at the table. It's like the dog is playing the game."

"You feeling okay, though? Getting outside? It's so pretty there."

"It's hot. All the time, like an incinerator. Your grandfather loves it, but I stay in. Maybe you'll come soon. Can you come soon?"

I wanted to tell her yes, that we'd be there the next day. Though she saved the dying for calls with my mother, she still didn't sound like the robust and vibrant person I knew. Something was off.

She continued to contact Mom with similar reports, and I called back a few days after each one, wanting my inquiries to feel random. Sometimes, she told me that she was too tired to talk. Sometimes, we spoke about Belle Harbor or my crush on Charlie Rogers and how I did my hair. No one else knew about Charlie Rogers. Sometimes, Papa Sam said she'd call me back, but she didn't.

"Grandma Lilly needs us to come," I said to my mother.

"I told you, your father is always at the hospital now, day and night, and I'd like to sit down for once and take a break. I don't remember when we saw a movie."

"Well, someone should go. It doesn't have to be all of us."

"She's just being dramatic, but okay, I get it."

"I've been talking to her, and she sounds bad to me. Maybe you're used to it by now, but something's not right."

"Okay, enough."

"You need to do something and stop ignoring it."

"Jesus, Kate, you just don't quit."

During a free period at school, I went to talk with the librarian, Mrs. Henry. She knew me well, as I liked to read the magazines at the table by her desk.

"I want to find out why people get sad, really sad, depressed." She looked concerned. "Not me, don't worry. My grandmother."

"I'm so sorry, dear." She came around the desk and put her hand on my arm. "Follow me."

We walked to the psychology section, and she pulled out a few books and slid them back, one after the other, until she located a thick blue text, traced her finger over the index and flipped to the page.

"This should be a start," Mrs. Henry said. "It gives you some history. And come back if you need to talk about it."

I took the book home and stayed up past midnight reading the chapter on depression. I learned about the melancholic personality type, which came from too much black bile in the body, according to the ancient Greek philosopher Galen. That seemed pretty crazy. And I read about Emil Kraepelin, who in the 1800s figured out that a depressive state could come unprovoked from the person's psyche—a mania—or could be triggered by some external event, "such as the death of a loved one." I thought of the baby.

I kept reading about these events, learning that a guy named Albert Eulenburg named them in 1878—psychic traumas—and that Sigmund Freud believed that people could repress the memory of them, actually make them not part of their consciousness. And, this hidden memory, rather than the actual event, could make them hysterical at some point in their lives without anyone knowing it was the culprit.

I shivered. Was it possible that Grandma Lilly wasn't just homesick? Had she forced the baby's death into oblivion in order to survive all these years, only to have it destroy her now? Or was I too obsessed to see straight? Everyone said I was obsessed.

A few days later, my parents told me that they had decided to take a trip over the next school vacation. It was an effort for them to make the time, so my case must have been convincing. Ben and I offered to stay back, if it would be easier to arrange, but my parents thought that our absence might make Grandma Lilly anxious. That was the word that had become associated with Grandma Lilly. *Anxious.* Challenging the house rules had paid off. I had altered a course, and I hoped that it would prove significant. I hoped that it was not too late.

I read the entire book and three others from the school library, keeping my psychological hypotheses to myself.

TWENTY-TWO

ON THE PLANE, BEN snatched a miniature sausage off of his breakfast plate and stashed it in his shirt pocket. "You'll see," he said.

Papa Sam picked us up at the airport. His head was as brown as a coconut. "She wanted to stay home and prepare lunch," he said, before we could ask. Last time, Grandma Lilly had come, too.

He was now driving Cadillacs, and he had a green one. Hunter with a tan interior.

"How does it feel back there? Nice?"

"Wide," said Ben. "You can fit the whole shuffleboard team in here."

"It's got three-speed automatic transmission, the smoothest ride around." He cut the air with his arm. "Can't feel the road, not a jiggle, right?"

We grinned at each other in the back seat, having heard the same about every car before this one.

"Not a jiggle, Pop."

The hallways in The Hemispheres Condominium and Towers smelled like roasted chicken and Jean Nate body splash. We carried our suitcases down the corridor, walking along the white trellises emblazoned on the wallpaper. Every third one had a yellow parakeet perched on its arch. We stopped in front of the door and waited for Papa Sam to take out his keys. *The Goldmans* was engraved on a silver nameplate beneath the peephole.

Ben took the sausage out of his shirt pocket and stuck it into his ear. I was responsible for our presence in the hallway, my instincts having led us to Grandma Lilly's threshold, and my belly churned with anticipation. She must have heard us coming and pulled open the door before Papa Sam could insert his key into the lock. She stood, rigid, staring, her slippered feet stuck to the carpet. Still in a nightgown, at one in the afternoon, she hadn't washed her face or powder-puffed her skin or applied the turquoise eye shadow and geranium lips, put on a fitted suit and charm bracelet and clip-on pearls. Her salon hairdo was crushed flat on one side and pushed into a bulge on the other, like the clumps of lambs wool I stuffed into my pointe shoes. The windows behind her cast her in shadow, outlining her form in a Florida glow. Saying nothing, she pulled at her fingers, left, then right, kneading them in front of her mouth. She spotted the breakfast meat jutting from Ben's ear and let out a howl, a warbly nightmarish squall that ripped through my stomach and into the hall, tracing the trellis arches one by one, like ocean waves when a boat goes down. She pressed the sides of her head and ran back into the light, disappearing into the bedroom at the end of the hall.

We stood in a row, breathless. Ben pulled the sausage out of his ear and grasped it in his fist.

Papa Sam stepped inside. "Come in, come in. She's just a little upset today."

"Jesus, Dad," my mother said. "What is going on?"

"Come, kids, don't worry," he said. "Here, let me take your things."

Ben put a hand on Papa Sam's shoulder. "I've got it."

"How long has she been like this?" Mom asked. "And why didn't you tell me?"

We stood in the foyer. Dad washed his hands in the kitchen sink. "Evie, take it easy. I'm going to go check on her. You kids okay?"

We nodded. The truth was, we weren't. Grandma Lilly's condition was far worse than what I could perceive on the phone. Up close, I didn't know what her behavior meant. Had some actual event or thought or fright caused it or was her body physically erupting, imploding on its own? Which would Albert Eulenburg choose?

I had learned about the circulatory system and the alveoli and the vertebra in the spine, and while a brain still soaked in formaldehyde on my bookshelf, I didn't understand its mysterious recesses. I dissected what it was made of, its material form, but I hadn't learned or come close to experiencing all that it could do, what its person could do and would do when the neurons shot this way or that, no matter how many library books I read. But I believed in intuition, and in this case, the science gave it credence.

The apartment was neat and clean. Tasseled pillows lined up at attention on the sofa, its cushions fluffed high in three mounds. The vacuum's path was carved into the carpet.

Mom paced around, muttering that she couldn't believe what was going on. Papa Sam said that she had been a little depressed lately.

"She called you, saying she was going to die," I said. "Why is this such a surprise?"

"She wasn't serious," my mother said.

"No, she wasn't," Papa Sam agreed.

"People don't say that. This is so infuriating."

"Relax, Kate," my father said.

"There are theories, you know, about depression." We walked into the living room, the ocean rippling out the window. "I've read about them. Bad memories can cause it."

"I think she probably misses New York," Dad said, looking at me intently.

The avoidance was overwhelming, and in the face of my grandmother's condition, I had had enough of it. "She has hysteria. Look at her. It could be psychic trauma, from something that happened a long time ago."

"Don't, Kate," he said.

"It could be from the baby. From not dealing with the baby." The words hung in the Florida air. "There, I said it."

"Kate," my mother yelled. "Stop it right now. This minute."

Papa Sam put his hand to his mouth and shook his head, sitting down on the couch.

"I'm sorry, Papa."

"You think everything's about that," said Ben.

"Well, maybe everything is."

"You are unbelievable, Kate," my mother said, sitting next to her father. "Are you okay, Dad?"

Papa Sam squeezed the corners of his eyes, saying nothing.

My father took me by the arm across the room. "Was that necessary? Can you tell me what good you thought that could do?"

"Repressing memories leads to suffering. I read every book in the library. Freud says you have to confront them or this happens."

"Go find her," Mom called to Dad from the sofa. She had her arm around Papa Sam. "Please, go check."

My father put his hands on his hips. "Maybe, but not like this. Not by you. You can't just read books and think you're a doctor when you're fifteen. It's irresponsible."

He walked quietly down the hallway to the bedroom. "It's Richard, may I come in?" He cracked open the door, a physician entering a patient's room.

I had thought that I was supposed to read books and do well in school and learn things so that I could find answers and figure out mysteries and make the world better. I knew that what I said could upset Papa Sam, but continuing to ignore it would be worse. I was disappointed that my father didn't give me the credit for weighing the consequences.

We couldn't hear anything else, from where we were in the living room.

"I didn't mean to upset you," I told my grandfather.

"I know," he said, finally.

Ben still clasped the sausage in his fist. He threw it out in the kitchen pail.

"What's that?" said Mom, holding her father's hand.

"He took a sausage from the plane and stuck it in his ear at the door," I said.

"How could you do that?"

"I thought it would be funny."

"It's all right," said Papa Sam. He smoothed his head and forced a smile. "Now, who's thirsty?"

Dad stayed in the bedroom for nearly an hour. Papa Sam gave us Diet Rite soda in glasses printed with orange slices. Too tall for juice.

"She picked out some clothes, and we're all going to take a walk," Dad said when he came out. "Why don't you go in and help her, Eva."

My mother hesitated.

"Go ahead, Evie," said Papa Sam.

Dad kissed her cheek. "Just be the way you normally are. But calmer. And nicer." He chuckled.

Dad asked Papa Sam questions about Grandma Lilly's recent behavior. This was the most extreme reaction that he could report.

"We'll figure out a plan while we're here. I think we can turn this around."

"What's your opinion?"

"I think she's a little homesick," Dad said, holding Sam's shoulder.

If this was true, it was because Papa Sam had asked her to leave her home. If she missed her only child, and us, and her life in Belle Harbor, it was because Papa Sam had wanted to move. My father knew that spelling this out would hurt Papa Sam, a generous man who thought he was giving his wife all that he could, tied up in a chiffon bow. But he had to say something. I suspect that Papa Sam already felt guilty enough, making all the days perfect, the sunshine pristine, the sofa cushions as fluffy as the Waldorf's. How we protect the ones we love. How we sacrifice for the ones we love. How we reconcile regret.

I believed that Grandma Lilly was indeed homesick, and seeing us all lined up in her doorway lit the psychological match. We were a reminder of what was taken from her, again.

Over the years, I had asked my parents for more details about the infant's death. By high school, the incident was no longer frightening, but it became more intriguing. It felt integral to our family's trajectory. Beyond my grandparents, I sensed that it had repercussions for all of us, spindly tentacles that wound in and around us, twisting us up. My parents told me all that they knew, which was what I knew from the start. They hadn't discovered more or seemed to want to.

Mom appeared in the hallway with Grandma Lilly, who had chosen a navy-and-white striped shirt dress, belted at the waist, and white sandals. Her hairdo was now centered on her crown, though the tendrils that framed her face couldn't deny their prior tumult. Carnation pink was drawn upon her lips, a stamp of resilience. A basket handbag hung from her forearm.

I walked slowly to her and extended my arms. Mom slipped away, and my grandmother and I hugged, her hands trembling on my back.

———————

We took the footbridge over the main road to the beach, where a promenade extended for miles. Grandma Lilly wanted to stay closer to the apartment building, but Dad insisted we walk along the water. A man who relied on quantitative information, he believed, too, in the influence of one's surroundings on spirit and well-being. In the operating room, he cut with scalpels and scissors, tied catgut into knots. Repair was mechanical, informed by data, but not without instinct. If intervention had stopped the forward progression, healing of a physical wound occurred microscopically, after fourteen days. But mending the psyche eluded such a fix. It was all instinct, and it required compassion and understanding, distant horizons and contented gulls. Grandma Lilly did whatever Dad advised, having chosen him originally for his wisdom and reliability. Her trust in him only grew with the years.

She walked ahead with my parents, her sandal buckles blinking in the sun, like sparks. The steps were slow. "Breathe that salt air, kids," Dad said, glancing back at us. "Expand those lungs."

I looked out toward the sea, aqua and cornflower and teal, translucent. Waves curled into the shore, speaking the maternal language, soothing discomfort, easing the unknown. Papa Sam walked between Ben and me, linking arms.

"I'm so sorry," I said.

He patted my hand and kept pace, his cap refusing the sun, cigar crinkling in his sock.

Twenty-Three

MY FATHER ARRANGED FOR Grandma Lilly to see a psychiatrist, and for the next few months, she seemed stable. Papa Sam also kept us better informed, which helped us feel more secure from far away. Grandma Lilly participated in activities and social occasions and even volunteered twice a week at the hospital gift shop, a place that had provided purpose in the past. On the phone, she sounded more vigorous and optimistic.

My parents visited once during that time, finding Grandma Lilly's condition much improved under a doctor's care. She and Papa Sam planned to come north for my Sweet Sixteen and would stay with us for some days before and after. About a month ahead of the party, a fancy affair held in a room at a restaurant, a large manila envelope arrived in the mail. In it was a note from Papa Sam, accompanied by fabric swatches in a flurry of colors and types and pencil drawings of dress designs.

Dear Kate,

I would like to make you a beautiful dress for your birthday. Choose a style, two colors and two kinds of fabric for each. One of the satins, taffetas or crepes can go under, and a sheer can be the overlay, if you want one. It can be a solid color or a combination of the two, whatever you like. Your grandmother and I can't wait to see you.

Love,
Papa Sam

I spread out the cuttings on the dining room table, and Mom came in to see. "So what do you think?"

"This is the best. I can't believe it."

"You know your grandfather. He wanted you to have the prettiest dress ever made. After you pick, we'll call him with your measurements."

"I think I like the shell pink. No, wait, the pale blue and the lavender, mixed. And definitely this style, the tea length. Maybe. Or this one. What do you think?"

"It's your choice, and you don't need any help. You've got a great eye."

I played with the swatches, moving them around the table in a multitude of permutations and combinations, and I studied the designs, imagining them in three dimensions. Papa Sam's sketches were stunning in and of themselves, the silhouette strong and clearly shaded, the details rendered precisely. They did a job, but they had whimsy. I wondered why I hadn't seen any of them framed and on a wall, and I decided right then to hang the drawings over my desk.

Angie walked into the room. "Is this the dress?"

"You knew, too?"

"Of course, I knew. Couldn't wait to see." She bent over the table to look. "You know which you like?"

"I can't decide. Which would you pick?"

"Oh, I'm not saying."

It took me a couple of days to visualize the options, to picture them at the party, hugging my friends at the door, filling with air on the dance floor, carrying themselves from the waist up while they sat for dinner. Papa Sam had drawn wildly different designs; he called me "a hanger," meaning that anything would fit over my hipless and barely breasted figure. From a creator of dresses, this was a supreme compliment, as I'd supply a form on which tailoring was a breeze. Later, people would say I had a *dancer's body*. I suppose that if I wasn't a dancer, I would have taken the term to mean that I was shapeless, just a collection of limbs, and I would have been insulted. But, since I was—actually—a person who danced, I considered the descriptor as something favorable, or decided to, anyway. *Well, thank you very much. I have worked hard as a dancer to have this body. You are so kind to notice.*

Among Papa Sam's designs, there was a shoulder-grazing bodice swathed in organza to the waist, where tulle shot out in all directions to the knee. Another had three-quarter sleeves, a boat neck and A-line pleats to the ankle. Still another had two-inch ribboned straps that crisscrossed down the length of the dress.

After careful deliberation, and some sketching of my own, I wondered if the top half of one could be paired with the bottom of another. Papa Sam determined that such a phenomenal variation could, in fact, be sewn, and so began work on a three-quarter-sleeved, boat-necked, dropped-waist, knee-length party dress in lavender and ice blue.

A week before the party, he, Grandma Lilly and the garment arrived in New Rochelle. I was relieved to see my grandmother, physically, standing in front of me, and also to see that she smiled and laughed and conversed. She seemed more tentative and a little foggy, but Dad said the medication could cause those effects.

Papa Sam unfurled the dress and snapped his wrists. The fabric floated, hung magically for a moment, and billowed to the floor. "There she is."

"Show the back," Grandma Lilly said.

He twirled it around, and she ran her hand from the neckline down. "Covered buttons, Katie." Her green eyes widened.

"It's the most beautiful dress I've ever seen."

They smiled at each other and huddled close. It had been a joint effort.

"Let's see how it fits," Grandma Lilly said. She was in charge of alterations.

She and I went into my bedroom, and she slipped the dress over my head. "All right, Sammy, you can come in now."

Mom and Angie followed.

"My word," Angie said. "Ya'll made something glorious."

"Just stunning," Mom said. "You outdid yourself."

"Your mother had a big part, you know. She's the artistic one."
Grandma Lilly blushed.

I spun on my toes and felt the skirt lift.

"I think it needs a cinch right here," she said, holding my arm to the side and inspecting the back of the neckline. "And what about the length? Do you like it a touch shorter, Sam?" She stood behind me and crouched, raising it up a half inch.

Papa Sam leaned on his back foot and rested his hand under his chin.

"Or as it is?" She dropped the hem and stood straight.

"Turn again, Katie," he said. "Slowly." Length affects the entire silhouette, so this was an important decision. "I like it as is. But let's take in the neckline like you said, just a tiny bit, eighth-inch, maybe. Otherwise, it's like a glove."

Grandma Lilly nodded and pressed her cheek into mine.

"I love it," I said, kissing her. "So much. Thank you."

Unlike the Spin-the-Bottle fiasco, I was in full control of this birthday's guest list. In the three years that had passed since I turned thirteen, more than half of the kids who surprised me in my basement discotheque had evaporated, either by choice or circumstance. This included Todd Forrester, I'm ecstatic to report, who, miraculously, left for boarding school after junior high. It became clear that the distance between thirteen and sixteen was cavernous. A veritable gorge of progesterone, interpersonal dramas about which boy liked which girl, who said what behind whose back, had rendered some previous acquaintances incompatible. Now, I had found the people who appealed to my dueling predilections for scholarship and solitude as well as for fun. Somehow, I had inherited qualities from each of my parents that could coexist in me, where they caused tension between my mom and dad. I could be playful and earnest, artistic and methodical, late and early, and figure out how, in one body, to come out straight, balanced and happy enough.

This is not to say that I wasn't still confused and discombobulated around boys to whom I was attracted. In my three years of teendom, as the other girls learned to flirt, to lead, to shut down and even to touch such male people, I became a squeamish mess, while also being present and noticeable in memorable outfits and mascara. I attended parties and school dances and had a wonderful time with my boy and girl pals. I presented myself coiffed and groomed, poised for attention, but I vaporized when someone wanted a closer look. The words for this, then, were *aloof, icy, coy* and no doubt other turns of phrase that were less polite. In my head, the terms were *shy, uncomfortable, young*. I was painfully aware that I felt tenuous in the midst of sexual tension, on the cusp, betwixt and between. I wanted to be as confident with the boys I thought were cute as I was in the rest of my life, but I didn't feel ready or know how to be.

"My sister didn't kiss a boy until college," Nanette said. "You're like her."

"What happened when she did?"

"She broke out. Zits all over."

"You're joking."

"Actually, no, she really did, the first time. Then she was okay."

My crush on Charlie Rogers had grown with me, and I invited him to the party. During the three years in which I observed him from across classrooms, tennis courts and cafeterias, he proved to be considerate, tempered and witty, all of which lassoed my imagination and whipped it into uncharted terrain. Infatuated, I watched him interact with other people—effortlessly, blithely—envisioning the other people to be me. From behind textbooks in the library and music stands in the flute section, I telescoped my sights on Charlie Rogers, on the essence that was Charlie Rogers, never once conniving or expecting a response, as the view from afar was simply enough to navigate, and simply enough. It felt that we had communicated when we clearly hadn't, and that was entirely sufficient. So, it seemed appropriate to invite him when maybe, it was ridiculous.

"The phone's for you," my mother called from downstairs. "A boy."

My brother and I shared the hall phone outside of our bedrooms.

It had an electrical cord that could reach California. I pulled it into my room and closed the door.

It was Charlie Rogers. "I can come to your party. Sounds cool."

I collapsed to the floor and covered my eyes. "Great."

"So I can get a ride with Dan. He's going, right?"

"Great, yes, and he lives near you," I said, cringing as the words sailed out of my mouth, realizing he'd think I was tracking his whereabouts. "I know that from the invitations, from writing them, so..."

"Cool. Yeah, you have crazy handwriting...so, thanks for the invite. See you in math."

"Great. Okay, bye."

He knew I was in math.

"You know," Ben said, opening the door. "You said 'Great' three times.'"

I stood quickly and gathered up the phone cord.

"Something tells me you were nervous," he continued.

"Something's telling you the wrong thing."

"It's not like you to repeat words. And words like *great*. Who was it, anyway?"

"No one."

"You like him."

"Can you leave now?" I pushed him on his arm.

"It's not a bad thing to like someone, you know."

"I don't like someone, and I have homework."

Ben was entirely comfortable with girls. I'm not sure how that happened, birthed as we were from the same genetic soup. Same access to Piaget's theories on cognitive development. It was confounding, but I loved him anyway.

Nana Sofie was now living with Aunt Eleanor and Uncle Roger, as she needed help with most daily tasks. They arrived in New Rochelle a little bit before we were due to leave for the party.

Aunt Eleanor gave me a copy of James Joyce's *A Portrait of the*

Artist as a Young Man. "He comes of age. You'll see."

In the books that she gave me, Aunt Eleanor synchronized the protagonists' developmental stages with mine. When I was eight, she gave me Johanna Spyri's *Heidi*, not because I would head into the mountain passes to live with a reclusive grandfather, but because Heidi was in the throes of discovering herself. Aunt Eleanor had no idea that my mother had just told me about my dead baby uncle, so Heidi's predicament—an orphan sent off to live with an aunt who deposits her with a crotchety old man—had particular resonance. Wanted babies lost, unwanted babies found.

Nana Sofie reached into her purse and pulled out a small box, wrapped in paisley paper. I opened it to find a delicate amethyst ring.

"It was my mother's," she said. "Your great grandmother's. She had intuition." She gave me a knowing look.

"It's the exact shade of the dress," Papa Sam said.

I slipped the ring on and off my fingers until it found a home, the third one on my right hand. I touched the stone and felt my great-grandmother, and her grandmother, and all the others who came before whom I didn't know, or know enough about. There they all were, in my living room, in my sinew and bones.

Nanette was my first guest. She did not come alone. She went nowhere alone. In her case, an entourage was not a sign of insecurity but rather a testament to her status and likability, exemplary, both. This is not always the case among teenage girls. Inhabiting the top social tier typically implied "popularity," which parades as likability but is wholly different. Popularity has an underbelly. Coercion, subjugation, obliteration of self. It is sinister.

Nanette was not popular and didn't care to be, which is why she was adored. She arrived with Susie Harmon and Billy Sloate, who sought me out after I slept under the forsythia by their merged backyards seven years earlier. I suspect that at first, they were merely curious, or disobedient—"Stay away from that Nichols girl," their parents told them, they later revealed. But they were impressed by my running away. More impressed that I did it at night. Their intrigue led to friendship, as so often it does.

It hadn't occurred to me then that news of my disappearance would circulate through the suburban airwaves, causing my classmates to question my emotional stability. When Susan and Billy told me months later that it had, I was confused about how I thought I was perceived. Was I now the Troubled Girl or the Weird Girl, when before, I was the Smart Girl? It was impossible to be more than one kind of Girl.

By sixteen, though, the episode had retreated to the collective background, as I had proven myself to be of sound mind in the years since. And, as they mutated into adolescents and later fully seasoned teens, the kids gave me leeway, chalking up the escapade to childhood immaturity, unaware that I fled because of something much more serious, that some unknown circumstance threatened the existence of my family. In the interim years, I vowed to myself to never inquire again about the situation, to never hunt for clues in file cabinets or interview my relatives, for fear of uncovering something treacherous and then having the decision about what to do. I wasn't ready to not have the family I had. But the information lived inside me, dormant. I was able to put it away, to zip it in a pocket, thinking that one day, in a different time and place, I would dig it out of hiding. I would not allow it to become a repressed memory.

"Oh my God, the balloons," Nanette squealed, throwing her arms around me. "And the dress...I can't believe your grandpa made this. Lavender is Charlie's favorite color, you know."

My face flashed hot.

"Don't worry, he's clueless. Only I know, and Susie."

"And Lauren," Susie said. "I told Lauren."

"Oh god, how did you guys know? I didn't say a thing to anyone."

They laughed and rolled their eyes, shadowed in frosty drugstore pink.

"C'mon, everyone's almost here," said Nanette, linking my arm. "This is so fun!"

Within minutes, the room was full. Weeks before the party, Mom had projected a photo of my face onto a huge square canvas and traced the key features, filling in the lips with red paint and the eyes, light brown. My friends wrote flattering and inspirational messages to me in the background—"I'm so glad you sat next to me in Mademoiselle Stone's French class," "You are destined for success,"—except for the Morris twins, who signed their names on my cheeks. Tommy on one side; Timmy, the other. The inscriptions looked like sutures if you stood back a couple feet. A lucky slashing victim, or a bout with cystic acne, post-op.

Charlie Rogers entered with little fanfare, slipped in, hands in his pockets. Nothing beats a navy sportcoat kicked back by pocketed hands. I started to count before crossing the room and greeting him, despite my position as hostess, which nullified the need to delay for cool's sake. For I-don't-have-a-crush-on-you sake. As hostess, I was supposed to be enthusiastic and welcoming. I was supposed to hurry right over and smile and usher him inside.

"Greet every guest and take the coats," my father had taught me when I turned three. "And at the end, show them out. They should never leave by themselves." Before anyone came or went, he swept the porch.

I checked myself in a mirror and walked toward Charlie. He looked at my dress when he saw me. I wondered if lavender really was his favorite color.

"Hey, thanks for coming. Did you get a ride with Dan?"

His hair, longish and parted on the side, was damp. He had showered within the hour.

"He had to do something first, so I got dropped off. But he'll be here pretty soon."

"Well, come on in. Almost everyone's here."

I detected a botanical scent, maybe a cucumber.

"Cool," he said, taking a gift from his jacket pocket. "You look really nice, by the way. And this is for you. My sister picked it out."

If I had the ability right then to assess our exchange, I may have noticed several significant, if not startling, indications. First, he looked at my body and later commented positively about it. Second, he chose to come on his own, without Dan, a decision that could reasonably imply that he did not want to be late. Third, he showered. And fourth, his choice in gift was meaningful enough to him that he enlisted his sister's help. Certainly, a person might enlist his sister's help if he did not care what was contained in the box or want to spend his time hunting for it, but unless he had malicious intent or was a passive-aggressive narcissist, he wouldn't divulge this lack of interest to the giftee, I wouldn't think.

Of course, I made none of these observations at the precise moment of our meeting at the party door, distracted as I was by the flung-back sportcoat and wafts of cucumber pulsing from his moistened locks. To me, he was a boy I liked, not one who liked me back.

We walked into the room, and I peeled off. James Taylor drifted from the speakers.

During the course of the party, I kept an eye on Charlie from afar, as I was in the habit of doing. Something seemed different, though, across this room, beyond my dressed-up friends and pink plaid tablecloths. I sensed that it was possible that Charlie Rogers could actually feel something for me, too, and this time, I didn't cast off the thought. Was sixteen an age to be daring? Bold? To believe in one's potential? Or was being the center of attention merely going to my head, momentarily, like a coma victim who pops back into lucidity for a precious visit, only to regress.

I found Nanette by the buffet. "I think he's going to ask you to dance."

"You do? When?"

She turned around and spotted him. "Soon. Within minutes. Just be available, and don't run away."

"Oh, god, do I look okay?"

"The prettiest ever. Even your boobs."

"Had to wear a bra with this dress. A real one."

Meantime, I spun around the dance floor with the other boys, none of whom made my belly flutter or tongue flop. The party was to end at eleven, and it was nine-thirty. Stealthily, I perused the perimeter of the room, failing to find Charlie anywhere. He wouldn't have left, but could he have meandered down the hallway or gone outside, bored? Oh, god, Kate, confidence. You're sixteen. He might even like you.

The song ended, and a slow one kicked in. "Muskrat Love." The boys made quick exits, and I turned to walk off the dance floor, too.

"I love this song. C'mon." Charlie Rogers appeared in front of me, his Oxford sleeves rolled up, tie loosened.

In seconds, his hands curved around my waist, feeling firm, but not stiff. His fingertips pressed into my back. I lifted my arms to his shoulders, glancing into his eyes and looking away. We stepped side to side, swaying, air between us. It felt that I was smiling too much, so I tried to rein in my lips, tensing them at the edges.

"The party's really fun," he said. "I like the drawing."

"Thanks. My mom traced it from a photograph."

"It looks like you."

I decided that it was not cucumber, but something woodsy, like pine or cedar. He stepped closer. Then he took one of my hands and raised it, turning me underneath in a slow pirouette and reeling me back in.

"Wait, you take dance, right?"

I nodded.

He spun me again, two times. "I bet you can do a million of these."

He moved his hands higher up my back. My muscles softened; my breaths deepened. My chest grazed his. The room turned around me, a carousel. A blur, anchored by random images, clear pictures that reminded me where I was. The birthday cake, frothing in flowers, at three o'clock. Susie Harmon chatting up a group of girls, at six. Ben, at nine, flirting with Mimi Greenhouse.

At one of the corners of the dance floor, my family sat at a table. Angie had come, too, along with friends of my parents, a couple they had known for years. I lifted my fingers off of Charlie's shoulder and waved to Grandma Lilly, but we turned before I could see her response. On the next revolution, I expected her to be ready, to make some encouraging motion in reply, to fold her hands in front of her chin and cock her head, to bend an elbow and rock back and forth. Mimicking our slow two-step, sharing in my first welcome encounter with a boy, as she was still the only person I spoke with about such things. I waved again. But she didn't react. She gazed straight at me, seeming to see me but not acknowledging it. She was calm; her eyes were flat. I lifted my hand again, moving it side to side with more strength, more speed, pushing the air, clearing the dust.

Charlie pressed his chest against mine. My skin receptors, already on high alert, drank in the stimuli. I must have lit up red. A neon sponge, soaked with the stuff of attraction, the elation, the separateness, the hope.

On the third turn, Grandma Lilly repositioned herself in the chair, eradicating me from her line of sight. Papa Sam leaned to tell her something and then stood. It appeared methodical, familiar.

I gripped Charlie's shirt, pulling the cotton into my palm. He lowered his head, and his hair skimmed my cheek. The space between us shrank and grew warm. Too soon, the song wound down. Our movement slowed. He released me and stepped back.

Grandma Lilly's seat was empty.

Charlie Rogers' face was flush.

I smoothed out my lavender organza, a parachute, landing soft. Cooler air kissed my skin.

There was not to be, I was beginning to see, the beauty of one blissful sensation, felt singularly without interruption. There would be a pairing, an undeniable coupling of competing emotions. Exhilaration and worry. Anticipation and fear. Love and despair. One would not happen without the other. I stood on the dance floor, feeling life's wicked tug, realizing the weight—of choosing, of responding to one or the other—and also the importance of savoring the good.

"I want to sign your picture," Charlie said. He took my hand and led me to the easel.

Later that night, I told my father what I had noticed.

"There was so much activity, and you were across the room. Maybe she was thinking about something or distracted by what someone said. We were all talking a lot."

"It just hit me funny. The gaze."

He leaned back on the sofa and stretched his legs. "I'll take a look tomorrow. It could be from the medication."

"Thanks. And thanks again for the party. It was the best, ever." I kissed his cheek.

"I'm happy you had fun." He shook out his newspaper. "She's seeing a doctor, Katie. So don't worry."

I fell asleep under Fifi and Gigi, replaying the dance with Charlie, wrapping my own arms around my back, analyzing each sentence that he spoke. Though it had been a while since I had talked with the can-can girls on my bedroom wall, that night, they got an earful.

Twenty-Four

A FEW MONTHS LATER, Papa Sam called my mother to tell her that he was going to the hospital for monitoring. He had experienced tightness in his chest and would be undergoing a battery of tests, requiring that he be admitted for two to three days. The echocardiogram showed no evidence of a heart attack, fortunately, but we were still concerned. He was seventy-seven and rarely had a sniffle, but chest discomfort is one of those fickle symptoms. You could have eaten too much shredded wheat, or you could be dead in an hour.

"Should we book you a flight?" Dad asked my mother.

"Now? There's not enough time."

"When are you going to go, then?" Ben asked.

"I don't know. When it's necessary."

"It's not necessary?"

In 1976, people booked plane tickets months in advance. Flying was a production, an adventure in and of itself. But my grandmother now had a psychological history, despite how stable she recently appeared. A hospital procedure was stressful, and it was new. My dad had cases he couldn't reschedule, but my brother and I couldn't understand how my mother could stay home. Only one person needed to be with Grandma Lilly.

"You'd go, right?" Ben asked me.

"Of course, I'd go."

Ben squinted. "Typical Mom. She doesn't get it when people need things."

Grandma Lilly drove Papa Sam to the hospital and stayed until he was settled in his room. She returned home in the late afternoon, before dark. I called her that night to see how she was doing. Ben and I took turns talking with her.

"He's going to be home in a couple of days," she said. "He's going to be all right, playing his shuffleboard. He loves that shuffleboard, boy oh boy."

"He's so good at it," Ben said. "Strategic."

"*It's in the strategy.* He says that all the time."

"Yeah, you've got to block the other guy. That's how you win." Ben passed me the receiver.

"He's going to be okay," I said.

"Where's your mother?"

"You want to talk to her?"

"She's probably busy, but she'll call me later."

"I can get her."

"She'll call me later. She's busy."

I motioned to Ben to find Mom and kept Grandma Lilly talking while he got her. He came back a few minutes later, alone, shaking his head. We hung up and returned the phone to the hallway table.

When I woke up the next morning, I called to check on her. The phone rang and rang. I got ready for school and dialed again before leaving.

"Don't worry about me," she said, finally answering, her voice trailing off. "You be good." She hung up before I could say anything else.

My father had already left for the hospital, and Mom was about to walk out. I caught her in the den by the garage door. "Grandma sounds weird to me. I just called her. Can you get someone to check on her?"

"What do you mean? Hurry, I'm late."

"I don't know, but she sounds out of it. Isn't there someone in the building you can call? That neighbor?"

"I suppose, but I can't now. After school, I'll do it. I can't dig up the number, I'm so late." She whisked out the door and into her car.

I called four-one-one from the den phone and got the number for The Hemispheres Condominium. Ben came downstairs, ready to walk to the bus stop. "C'mon, we'll miss it."

I wanted to call from home but had no other way to get to school. I checked to see that I had dimes in my wallet for the phone booth outside the cafeteria. We said goodbye to Angie and headed for the corner.

———————

At lunch, I reached someone in the condominium office.

"I sent someone to check on her this morning," the woman said.

"What do you mean?"

"Someone called. Wait, I wrote it down. Angie. A woman named Angie called."

I leaned on the phone booth wall, relieved.

"And your grandmother was okay, so don't worry."

"Can you check again?"

"I'm the only one here, but I can go on my break. In forty-five minutes."

"You can't go sooner?" It had been four hours.

"Sorry, but I can't leave."

"I'm going to call you back after school." Billy Sloate banged on the door of the booth. "Or my mom will." I thanked her and hung up.

"You okay?" Billy asked.

"Worried about my grandmother."

"That stinks," he said and ran down the hall.

———————

That evening after dinner, Papa Sam called while Ben and I were doing homework. I heard Mom answer in the den, down the hall. Then I heard a crashing, something breaking on the floor.

"Richard!" she yelled.

We opened our doors. Mom ran toward us and picked up the phone outside our rooms. Dad was on the other receiver.

"Talk to him," she yelled toward the den. "Say something. He's standing there all alone."

My father had been in touch with Papa Sam's doctors during the thirty-six hours that he had been in the hospital. He was stable, and infection had been ruled out. It was likely that he had angina, which would have to be treated medically and watched. He was due to be discharged the next afternoon, so I couldn't figure out what would have caused the dropped vase, the running, the hysteria.

"Richard, say something," she hollered again, falling into the chair and doubling over.

Ben and I slid past Mom and walked into the den, where our father was standing away from his desk, avoiding the glass on the floor. He motioned to us to stay back. I went downstairs to get a broom and dustpan from the laundry room. When I returned, the phone call was over.

"Put on shoes to do that," Dad said, rubbing his forehead.

"Can you tell us what's going on?" Ben asked.

Mom still sat on the chair at the other end of the hall, bent in half, rocking.

Dad explained that Grandma Lilly went into a diabetic coma. She didn't take her insulin, and her blood sugar levels got too high, raising her risk for a pulmonary embolism, a clot in her lung.

"Where is she? Who found her?" I looked at Mom down the hall, palms on her face. "Is she not okay? Are you saying she is not okay?"

"They didn't get there in time," my father said. He stepped around the shards and walked toward us, helpless. He had said this before to families, approached them this way, with lowered eyes, solemnity.

I dropped the broom and hurried from the den before he got to me, racing outside to the yard. I ran through the grass, feeling my gut wrench, hearing my sobs hang in the night. I fell to my knees and pulled the grass, ripping it from the earth, clenching it in my fists. The floodlights shot on from above, uncovering my body like an escapee's, trapped in chopper beams. Get away, I called. She need-ed the lights, not me. She needed you, not me. Get away.

Ben appeared next to me on the lawn, sobbing.

"It wouldn't have happened if we made them go," I said. "We didn't do enough."

––––––––––

Ben and I later learned that our grandfather repeatedly called Grandma Lilly from the hospital phone, and when she didn't answer, he contacted the building management and the local police. They went to the apartment with an ax and broke through the door. Grandma Lilly was on the floor by the bed.

She had been injecting herself with insulin for thirty years, but she failed to take it when Papa Sam went to the hospital.

They didn't get there in time. We had plenty of time.

––––––––––

My mother flew to Florida. She helped Papa Sam pack a suitcase and brought him back to New York. His doctor prohibited him from attending his wife's funeral, a common practice then, maintaining that the stress would strain his weakened heart and risk his own demise. Dad examined him and agreed, weighing the physical impact of being in the chapel, seeing her laid out in blue lace, against the angst of missing the ritual. Both were agonizing and unfinished, but he believed, medically, that Papa Sam would be safer if he stayed back.

Trained in a doctor's house to accept the treatment without indulging the feelings it churned up, we didn't question the decision. Dad instructed Ben, who had determined to become a doctor, to stay at home with Papa Sam while he, Mom and I drove out to Belle Harbor for the ceremony.

That morning, Papa Sam put on a suit and crisp white shirt, intending to defy his physicians' orders or perhaps simply mark the day. I didn't ask which. He sat in the living room, in front of the picture window, sun streaming onto his tanned head. He wore a tie clip, his initials engraved in seriphed print.

"We'll have a service here, later," I said, hugging him.

He noticed that I was wearing the locket, and he opened it and touched the photographs.

"On the patio," I said. "She loved the patio."

He nodded, and we cried.

Ben sat down next to him.

"Put on a suit," I said.

When it was time, my parents and I drove off, leaving the two of them on the sofa, dressed up, awash in morning light.

PART THREE
2002

Twenty-Five

ROXY SCREAMED FROM THE car seat, grasping me with her four-year-old arms as I latched the clasp. She knew that I wouldn't be leaving our house and going with her, that it would be the first time we were to be apart overnight. Her father sat behind the wheel, ignoring his child's wails.

That my daughter needed to sleep that night at his apartment was a misguided and cruel notion, given her reaction. But Jeff, the man with whom I had fallen in love, trusted and married in my early thirties, insisted that she change into pajamas in his spare bedroom, brush her tiny teeth in his extra sink, and lay her head down on his stiff new sheets, speckled as they were with purple rabbits when she liked only cows. In North Carolina, family law supported this torture, unless, of course, reasonable parties agreed to another plan. Jeff was not a reasonable party.

When we married nine years earlier, I was certain that he was, and that he always would be. Ah, the slanted view. The cockeyed perspective. The delusions of love. Then, he would not have been a man who'd be tempted, who'd succumb to another woman's flirtations, if just once. He would step back, hold out a stiff arm, leave the dimmed office alone, relieved, resolute. Loyal and principled, but not naive, he'd have been prepared for such a proposition, as cliche as they'd become. Then, he would not have been a man to make his daughter hurt, so he could stake a claim or exert control.

I bent into his back seat and wrapped my arms around Roxy, pressing my cheek into hers. Taking a frightened child from her mother, for no reason that would be deemed good for the child, was indefensible. Taking a frightened child from her mother to satisfy some emotional need in an adult was heinous. I touched the clasp on her strap, wanting to unlock it, to release her into my chest and run back inside, to her books and dolls and drawings and us.

"*If you don't let her go with him,*" my lawyer had said, "*they could take her completely.*"

I heard the warning in my head, felt my ribs ache and skin shiver in the heat.

"*And don't malign him in front of the child.*"

I squeezed the words back into my throat.

"*The court hates that.*"

The presumption.

Suspended mid-air, on the edge of bursting, I hugged Roxy harder and told her that I was just a few blocks away and that I would be there in no time and that she would be okay and safe because she was a big brave girl. A big brave girl who made me proud, so proud.

She sobbed and shook, and I peeled myself away from her writhing frame, held her face in my hands and tried to smile, the feigned smile of maternal encouragement and optimism, tears blurring my sight. I closed the door, and the car pulled away fast, her palm pressing on the window, her fingertips white like pearls.

———————

Inside, I paced the length of the house, front to back, back to front. I felt nauseated and woozy, stopping to steady myself on the banister. Through the front door window, two children played on the lawn across the street. I watched them, jealous. August sun forced waves from the pavement, even at eleven a.m.

The woman who worked with Jeff at the investment bank had been to our house for a party before they had sex in a storage room behind his office. She had walked on the hardwoods, sat at my table with their other colleagues, thanked me for a lovely time. And she returned after they had sex in the storage room behind his office and before the encounter was revealed to me, though I sensed the act's residual effects slithering across my hardwoods, dripping off my dining chair, mocking me at the door.

"It happened just once," Jeff told me later, presuming that I knew. "And if it means anything, she initiated it."

"It means you are not only unfaithful. You are weak."

Jeff was the boyfriend who wouldn't do such a thing. There were others who would, who had, and these I quickly discarded, even mid-date at the hint of a hunch. Loyalty was everything. I gave it wholly, to Jeff, to my father, to family secrets that still lingered in me, dormant. Jeff begged for my forgiveness, saying that he would never stray again, and I believed that he wouldn't. I believed that he'd be forever remorseful and vigilant, that he'd overcompensate, even. But I couldn't stay married to a person who didn't see the consequences beforehand, who gratified himself first and thought second. You can't unbake a cake. And you can't tell a daughter to excuse a man who cheats. Heartbroken, I filed for divorce, sheltering Roxy from the aftermath my only concern.

I sat crying on the bottom step, her image in the car window all I could see, through opened eyes or closed. She wasn't simply sad or angry. She was afraid. She was scared of what was happening around her, to her, and I couldn't save her. I couldn't reverse course. I couldn't reach into the water and pull her out, dripping, gagging, but intact. Rescued. My job was to protect her, and I had failed.

Later, I took our dog Henry for a walk. Roxy had chosen him a year earlier on a visit to the local shelter. He licked her hand through the chain-link gate and perked the one ear he could raise. She was smitten.

When I had trouble with the lede to a story, I put on Henry's leash, knowing that by the time we'd return, I'd have the words worked out. When I didn't have an assignment on my mind, I'd come back with an idea for a new one. My feet were connected to my frontal cortex.

I had become a journalist and worked as a reporter for the Raleigh paper. The profession made good use of my instinct and thorough nature.

Henry led me down the front path to the sidewalk, hopping over the massive tree root that had burst through the stone. We had been conditioned to step over it, and when guests arrived, we called from the door to warn them, prompting funny raised knees and ballet-ic leaps. Once, when my mother was visiting from New York, she went looking for a workman down the street and returned with a mason, powdered in white like a cookie. He wanted fifteen hundred dollars to repair and level the fissure, an amount that Jeff and I thought was excessive. We thought that acclimating to the hazard made better financial sense.

Henry took me to "The Shady Park," Roxy's favorite. Huge white oaks covered the playground, keeping the swings cool. Not a climber, she preferred to hang on and soar, taking turns with the dolls she brought from home, whom she secured in the seat and pushed. Henry tugged me inside the park, but I pulled him back to the sidewalk.

As we walked, I remembered my swing set in New Rochelle, and how one leg of it would jump up out of the ground if we flew too high, making the lub-dub of a beating heart. A breeze blew dust into my eyes, and I pictured a backyard birthday, chomping marshmallows off strings, tying ankles with strips of fabric and rac-ing three-legged across the lawn. I saw Grandma Lilly and Papa Sam, watching from the picnic table, and I saw their baby crashing to the floor.

I snapped my head left, right, jolted from a trance. The image stopped me cold. I had lost track of the route, the time, the present and didn't know where I was. Disoriented, I meandered for a block until Henry pulled me toward a street sign...Berry Road. Suddenly, I felt reeled in from the cosmos, magnetized to a geographic coordi-nate at lightning speed.

I was standing in front of Jeff's apartment.

Twenty-Six

I LED HENRY HOME at speed. Point A to Point B, crossing streets and lawns on the diagonal, keys shaking in my pocket. Inside, I threw my sunglasses onto the foyer table and ran up the steps to my desk. On a legal pad, I scrawled notes, whatever I could remember. Names, towns, birthdays, addresses. The computer revved up. The screen flashed blue.

Three decades after first hearing about the death of my uncle, I began investigating. I suspect, now, that having Roxy ripped from me in our driveway set off the part of my brain that responds to loss, to the loss of helpless babies in particular. My grandmother's trauma and its repression had been passed to my mother, who had followed the script and squelched the truth, the pain, the reality of what had happened, without concern for the consequences. And it had been passed to me, becoming embedded in my psychological makeup. As a child, I had attempted to break the pattern, to uncover the details as best as I could. I was not yet emotionally baked, not as clear in my thinking as I had become with age. But I had now felt similar trauma, shared the unbearable and horrific threat of losing a child—to something—and I was driven by some subconscious need to dismantle the previous practice, to hold a club to it and hit hard.

In the search bar, I typed my grandparents' names and assorted words...child, birth, Belle Harbor, death. I added a range of dates, 1927-1934.

The computer directed me to databases for birth and death certificates, but without the infant's full name and more specific dates,

I couldn't locate the documents. For hours, I sat at my desk, hunting for anything I could discover about the family, trying to remember whatever I had been told as a child.

When Jeff and I first separated, the newspaper agreed to let me work from home during the hours Roxy wasn't in pre-school. It was a mad dash each day, dropping her off and racing downtown to the office or out on a story, skipping lunch and sprinting back by two-thirty. I figured out what part of the work was best done where, and while the schedule was jammed, it was well worth it. At four-thirty, without looking at a clock, I made a natural migration to the kitchen to prepare dinner for Roxy.

I got up from my desk and took my pad and pen. There would be no slicing of carrots and apples, no baking of chicken. No food faces with eyes of peas and spaghetti hair. I took Roxy's lunch sack from the pantry shelf and gave it a good scrubbing, setting it out to dry on the counter. It was Saturday, but I could get her snacks ready for Monday. I could prepare them for school, as all mothers do, spooning raisins and cheese crackers and cereal flakes into a cellophane bag, zipping it tight. Writing a note. Drawing a flower and a heart. I could do all that two days ahead, of course I could.

I stood at the counter and made a list: Department of Records, Census Bureau, Hospital. Then I called Roxy on the phone.

"Do you think it's a good idea to upset her again?" Jeff said. "She's finally calmed down."

I logged what he said in the spiral notebook I had kept for months, recording his comments and actions. This prevented me from responding to his remarks, which, as this one did, left me incredulous and incensed in so many ways.

"Please put Roxy on the phone."

"If I must."

Roxy told me that she had noodles for dinner, and chicken and green beans. She said that her father might get a dog.

"I'm sorry that you were sad in the driveway," I said.

"I was sad."

"I was sad, too."

"There's a bear here, on my bed. A big one. And I'm going to sleep with her."

"That will be fun."

"Can you see her?"

"Tomorrow. I'll come see the bear, and then we'll go home."

"To my room?"

"To your room."

We spoke for a little while longer, after which I put away the boxes of crackers and cereal. I didn't know how I would be able to let Roxy go, routinely, for years. For fourteen years, until college. People said that it would get easier, but I didn't want it to or think that it should. It should never be easy for a mother to send her child away, anywhere, good or bad. That was not something to hope for or aspire to.

I dialed my own mother in New York.

"Was wondering about something…what hospital were you born in?"

"Queens General, why?"

"No reason, just curious." Mom was not one to delve.

My grandparents wouldn't have gone back to the same place for my mother's delivery, so I could rule this one out. Back at the computer, I located it on a map and drew a circle around it, figuring that their apartment on Ocean Parkway was within a five to ten-mile radius. Without a census report, I couldn't be sure of the exact address on this long road or whether they lived in the same home when the earlier baby was born. But they wouldn't have moved far and were likely in the vicinity, which was good enough.

I could have called my mother back and asked if she remembered hearing where her brother was born, a consequential detail. But I didn't want to reveal that I was researching the incident. This wasn't just an unsolved mystery; it was a way to understand the pathology of the secret, the way it changed my grandmother and formed my mother, making her the kind of parent that she was, and perhaps, the kind of daughter that I was. In uncovering the truth, I'd keep myself from becoming another casualty, if I wasn't, in some ways, already one. The power of the memory was a wallop. My mother would be the last interview, after I had the facts in front of me. This was a well-learned reporting strategy: she was the culprit, who when confronted with unarguable evidence of the crime, would have to confess.

That evening, I searched for old maps of Belle Harbor, trying to determine which other hospitals operated at the time and learning about the records that institutions keep and for how long, realizing that no witness would be alive for me to contact. I could hope for a descendant of a witness, someone who may have heard talk, but tracking down such a person would be a feat, particularly from Raleigh. I had come to the story late. It was no longer a rescue, but a recovery.

On-the-ground reporting, talking with long-time residents, would be the way to stumble on such a source. It was also the way I, and other reporters at the time, had been conducting our work, pretty much exclusively, as Internet research was just establishing itself in the early 2000s. We called, showed up at doors, watched with our own eyes. For documents, we'd go to libraries, government agencies, wherever the information may have been stored.

I discovered that three hospitals, including Queens General, existed within an eight-mile radius of Belle Harbor. I found photographs of the two in question. The first, Marine Memorial, was seven miles to the north, across Jamaica Bay in Brooklyn. It was a red brick building with white trim around the windows and heavy wood doors. My grandparents were born in Brooklyn and lived there when they were first married, so they likely had earlier connections to its hospitals. But having moved across the bay to the peninsula, Papa Sam would not have wanted to rely on a bridge while his wife was in labor. That route, with potential delays or closings, would not have been a prudent choice. Marine Memorial was not an option.

The second hospital, St. John's Episcopal, was closer, six miles east and a straight shot on Rockaway Beach Boulevard, past the high school that my mother would later attend. Established and operated by the Catholic church in 1905, it was first called St. Joseph's. Patients paid one dollar a day, if they could afford to. In 1976, as large healthcare corporations began to emerge, the hospital was taken over and renamed. I found two photographs of the original facility. One showed the front façade–a pale pink stucco, red tile roof–the other, a room inside. The room inside was, of all places, the nursery.

There, a nurse stood before a row of empty bassinets, holding two babies, one in each arm. This was the room. I knew that this was the room. The photograph was dated underneath, "circa 1934." My mother was born in 1935. This could have been the nurse.

TWENTY-SEVEN

IT WAS NEARLY TWO in the morning when I fell asleep. Still, I woke up at six-thirty, conditioned by Roxy's schedule. I had tried to extend her bedtime, thinking that the adjustment might shift the cycle, but she rose with the chickens, ready to go, no less good-natured than she typically was.

That night without her at home, I slept on my side of the bed. After Jeff moved out, I experimented with new positions and locations...the diagonal, the middle, the reverse. Once in a great while when I was a kid, I slept backward, putting my pillow where my feet had gone, untucking the bottom of the blanket and slipping underneath. The curtains, the ceiling, the windows all looked crooked, and it felt as if I had gone elsewhere. It felt strangely adventurous.

I hadn't yet ventured to Jeff's side of the bed, not wanting to touch with my body where his had been. I had thrown out his pillow and bought new sheets, but the bed hadn't become mine, yet, entirely. Perhaps that was a process, too, that wends its own way. Feelings had taken a course. Shock, anger, hurt, disappointment. Perhaps the emotion associated with adopting the former mate's domain as one's own would happen on a clock, too. Maybe, Month Three. At Month One, I couldn't imagine it.

Henry was still sleeping on the chair across the room, his internal rhythm appreciating Roxy's absence. I waited until he said it was time to rise.

The hydrangeas that lined the front of the house were in full bloom. I had planted them in front of a low-lying stone wall that flanked the two steps to the sidewalk. Employing Grandma Lilly's trick, I dropped a penny into the soil by each bush, which accounted for how well they flourished, I liked to think. After our morning walk, I clipped two branches and put them in a vase on the kitchen table. Soon, at the end of summer, the bushes would need pruning.

———————

The nurse's face was turned to the side in the photograph, looking down at one of the babies. In profile, her nose was straight like a pencil. She wore a starched uniform and cap, which sat on top of a brunette bob, turned under, as was the style. If she was twenty-eight or nine in the picture, she would have been nearly a hundred years old in 2002. If she was not a nun and had children of her own, they could have been in their eighties or seventies, perhaps; grandchildren, even younger. If, while she was working, a baby fell to the tile and died, or became suddenly ill and died, such that the details of the situation were kept hidden from the parents, she would have told someone about it when she went home. She would have told a husband, if she had one, or a sibling or mother or father, if she lived with one. If she was a nun, which was probable, she would have shared the news with a Sister, under a garden arbor or in the refectory alcove, and they would have prayed. They would have prayed to make the bad event better, at least for them.

But, even if she told no one, having been instructed to say nothing, the knowledge of it would show on her face, as would the shame of deceit. At some point, someone would ask what made her look so. At some point, she would close a private door, lean back on it and whisper. She'd whisper, trembling, guilt-ridden, and pass on the lie—and the dilemma of what to do with it—to someone else. Someone in Far Rockaway, New York, knew what happened to my infant uncle. I was determined to figure out who.

I made a list of questions that I would ask the hospital the next day, Monday. First, the easy ones: How long are records kept? What happens when a new owner takes over? Are records ever destroyed? Are they given to patients first? And then the specific ones: Where is the original photograph? Is there a name written on the back?

How was it passed along from the Sisters of St. Joseph to you? What else do you have in your possession?

I realized that there would be only a death certificate filed with the state, given how few days the baby lived. When Roxy was born, I didn't receive her birth certificate until weeks later. There would not have been enough time to process the baby's paperwork, a disturbing notion to consider. But by law, hospitals need to provide a report for a death, which would contain a date for his passing. I did not expect it would list a particular cause, hidden from my grandparents as it was, or a name, as my mother never heard one mentioned and was certain none was given. My plan was to continue with the legwork until I had some solid data in my hands and could pursue a more aggressive line of inquiry.

That Sunday, while waiting to pick up Roxy, I researched the Goldman and Rosinsky families. States didn't have birth records until 1919, and since my grandparents were born in the early 1900s, I'd have to rely on census data for their vital details as well as those of their relatives, addresses, occupations and incomes. The New York census reports for 1930 and earlier were available on microfilm at various state archives, but not where I lived in North Carolina. The closest location would be in Washington, DC, four hours away. So, I printed out a form requesting the reports and put it in our mailbox for pickup. I had accomplished enough for the day.

A few weeks earlier, I had bought new ballet slippers for Roxy. Class would be starting that Monday, and elastics needed sewing. I took out the bag of thread from the hall cabinet and hunted for the dusty pink. Some of the spools were my mom's, used to make clothes for me, and some were the ones from Papa Sam's factory.

I inherited the collection when my mother cleaned out the back closet. The sewing had splashed firmly in my chromosomal stew and grown stronger over the years. Grandpa Leo's early skill as an upholsterer and my dad's mastery of suturing skin solidified the genetics on my mom's side. When Roxy's clothing repairs began to pile up, I bought my own machine, as my mom had done.

I folded the heel of the slipper to determine the correct spot for the elastic. Piercing through leather was not an easy job, and some brands came with the task already completed. But Roxy would wear the classic Capezios, despite the havoc they wreaked on my fingers. When I was finished, I returned the thread to the bag and sorted through its contents. At the bottom, I found a tin case of straight pins and a square of white tailor's chalk, most likely Papa Sam's.

I don't remember seeing any mother-of-the-bride gowns from his factory during my childhood. But my mom did describe them to me, saying that Papa Sam was exacting about the cut. "Fitted to perfection." I imagined them to be princess gowns, from the boxes of swatches, buttons and trimmings that he brought us from the factory.

I returned to my desk, and my hands typed "Lill-Dor Fashions." I waited for the computer page to load. One after another, dresses appeared on the screen, like playing cards flipped from a deck. Ice blue lace, tiered and ribboned at the waist. Pink chiffon with a handkerchief hem. Statuesque silk crepes that skim along to the hips and ripple to the floor. A seamstress had to have sat for hours beading the necklines by hand. Each had the signature label sewn inside, "A Lill-Dor Fashion" in claret-colored script across the diagonal, an art nouveau "New York" underneath. Some said "Reg," for the standard-size line.

Mesmerized, I envisioned my grandfather, bent over a work table in a white shirt, sleeves rolled up. Black-rimmed glasses. Five-seven frame, eight at most. I saw his calm, his concentration, his contentment. I saw his hands, small, agile, specific. The way he made a crease, holding it vertically in the air, pinching and pulling his fingers down evenly, decisively. Once, maybe twice. I saw him drape the pink chiffon, the ice blue lace, play with it on the dress form, gather it, fold it, pin it from the cushion on his wrist. Spin it on the model. Crouch and adjust a seam. I saw the shears, their fourteen inches, cutting through layers, his eyes and hands directing, smoothing, getting close.

I saw one dress...a froth of lavender and baby blue organza, a cousin of the Sweet Sixteen gift that he made for me. A scalloped V, tight waist, fantastically full skirt. A bow.

My grandfather was in my house, talking to me at my desk.

I read the captions and learned that the dresses were for sale on auction sites and in vintage shops across the country. I ran to my purse and got my wallet. It took some time, not ever having purchased anything this way before, but I bought the dress. I bought the lavender and baby blue dress, thinking that Roxy could wear it, that she could wear it and dance with a boy. That we just needed to have it close.

TWENTY-EIGHT

I RANG THE BELL and waited on the front step of Jeff's townhouse.

He swung open the door, wearing sweats and stubble. Roxy tore around the corner and slammed into me, where I crouched on the foyer floor. She gripped my skin with her tiny hands. She smelled like man soap. Sandalwood.

"I missed you every minute," I said, challenging the divorce psychologists who advise against saying something you used to say without anyone telling you not to say it. Wouldn't Roxy expect me to miss her? Wouldn't she want to hear me say it? I was relieved that she appeared intact.

"Me, too," said Rox. "Want to see the bear now?"

She led me to the bedroom where she had slept. I peeked in the closet and out the window. Jeff had hung the damask curtains that we used to have in the den. "Wow, she's huge. And very adorable."

Roxy gave the bear a hug—"Bye, Billie"—and turned to me. "That's her name."

I picked up Roxy's bag, and we left.

"Maybe a sheer for the sidelight," I said on the way out.

At home, we went out back to the yard to play a little before dinner, to breathe familiar air, to readjust, viscerally. Roxy rode her tricycle on the stone path, filling up the basket with twigs and leaves and dandelions. She enlisted Henry's help. "Find the treasures, Henry."

I sat on the porch step and rolled my head from side to side, extended my legs, flexed my ankles. The tension fell away. My muscles softened, melted into the wood under me. The feeling of high alert, of readiness for what I couldn't see, subsided. I was suddenly exhausted.

"Good boy, Henry." Rox organized her riches on the patio. "Look. Henry got lots of treasures."

———————

Later, Rox climbed into bed, having eaten her favorite sweet potatoes and fried eggs and bathed with strawberry bubbles, the sandalwood disappearing down the drain.

I planned to go to sleep early, too, beginning the evening routine, switching on the living room lamp and checking the doors. At my desk in front of a bedroom window, I straightened up papers and turned calendar pages and arranged my bag for work. Reaching for the power button on the computer, I hesitated and sat down, a new idea finding its way. I searched once again for the Goldman baby, typing, this time, instead of his parents' names, my mother's.

"Eva Nichols," "Eva Nichols brother," "Eva Nichols Belle Harbor." A few entries popped up, one listing the New Rochelle Public School District where she worked, another our address on Rolling Way. Toward the bottom of the page, I saw the word "obituary" and quickly clicked, not realizing that a newspaper wouldn't have written about the infant, but being drawn by the reference.

I blinked, opening my eyes to my father's face. Larger, clearer, brighter than the newspaper photo, the picture startled me, not ever having seen it this way, illuminated on glass, shiny. I touched his chin. I pulled my knees into my chest. I cried. That night, I left the computer on, his image like moonlight.

———————

Seven years earlier, my father passed away from cancer. Just sixty-one, he practiced medicine until three months before his death, not once uttering the name of his disease, despite the surgeries, the treatments, the tubes of oxygen running the length of the hallway upstairs. He told no one of his illness, allowing only Angie, who hadn't worked for our family in years, to come to the house to help toward the end.

"You have to follow his lead," she told Ben and me, and we did. We didn't say the name of the disease, either. We talked about my writing, his patients, the news of the day. We asked how he felt, as if he had experienced cold symptoms or a sore back. My mother, though, revealed his condition to anyone she'd meet. She'd tell them that she was overwhelmed.

Whether he avoided acknowledgement for him, for us, as coping, or instruction, or both, I don't know. I wanted to ask him those questions, though, those meaning-of-life questions that would clarify everything, make the tragedy make some kind of sense. I wanted to ask him if he was scared, or if he wanted to tell me something, anything, that I didn't yet know, that I would need to know. I wanted him to tell me that I was the best, so I could tell him the same. I wanted to tell him how much I loved him, but I couldn't. I wanted to tell him good-bye.

I had planned to use the first letter of my grandmother's name for Roxy. She was to be Lucy, for Lilly. Instead, we had to use the R. My father never met my daughter, and that irreversible, impossible fact launched a searing pain that lives in me, that flares with Roxy's every sentence, step, pirouette. Kindling on a fire.

My parents never disclosed the facts of the circumstance that they believed had threatened us, that sent me out into the night on my bicycle, raging, untethered. I had made a pact with myself, committing to leave it alone, sensing the gravity of it, even at such a young age. For thirty years, I kept the promise.

After my father passed away, I could have tried to find out what had happened without disappointing or exposing him. I wouldn't have had to confront him with the knowledge and watch him relive whatever it was, see his brows crease and lips tighten, hear his soles slap on the floor, tense and troubled. I was free to find out what he desperately didn't want me to.

It was not the first thought that I had after he died, not the twentieth, or the hundredth. His passing scorched me, left me ravaged like a tree after a fire. I was the young woman, then, whose father just died, the one who counted the days since. Since a former patient gripped my hand and cried, since I wiped the dirt from my good black shoes. Since the people brought candy and sat in our living room. I counted the months between surgeries, the admissions to the hospital, the hours the oxygen was used. I counted whatever could be put on a clock, before and after, after and before, a spin of data. How long would I do this, how many minutes, years, decades would I calibrate the absence? I was quantifying the pain, I suspect, now, giving it a form, an expectation. I didn't know, then, that it couldn't be done. I count, still.

Two years passed before I considered an inquiry. I was late in my pregnancy with Rox, up a lot at night, when the mind is a stunning ballet, ideas weaving and spinning, floating and leaping, forming patterns. I wondered about the secret, about what they and I had protected so well. It kept me awake, and I decided to confront my mother the next time I saw her and ask.

Before I had the chance, I went into labor and gave birth to Roxy, shifting life in all ways, instantly. A few nights after taking her home from the hospital, she and I woke for one of her feedings. We had a white bedspread, which I used to fold and put on a wicker chair before going to sleep. On top of it, I piled assorted decorative pillows, also white, a mountain of whipped cream. I woke up that night and saw my father floating above the bedding. From his vantage point, he would have been able to look down into the bassinet.

He was still too close. It was too soon. I left the secret alone.

TWENTY-NINE

THE MONDAY AFTER ROXY'S first weekend at Jeff's house, I drove her to preschool and walked her inside. "Ballet today?" she asked. She asked every day.

I nodded, kissed her goodbye and headed for the office. Before the newsroom got busy, I called the New York State Department of Records and provided whatever information I had. The man on the phone said he'd see what he could find and be in touch. Then, I called St. John's Hospital and was told that any documents they had saved from St. Joseph's at the time of the acquisition would have been long gone.

"One other thing," I said. "There's a photograph on your website of a nurse. Would you know if she is identified on the back of the picture?"

"Which photo?"

"The photo of the nursery, it's from St. Joseph's...do you have the original?"

The woman covered the receiver and muttered something about my questions.

"That photo is in our lobby. Can I take your name?"

If I were nearby, I'd drop everything, run to the lobby and lift the frame off the wall myself.

"Is there a way you can check it for me? Just take a peek at the back to see if there's a name?"

Muttering, again.

"I think it could be a relative of mine," I said.

"I'll see what we can do."

It was just eight-fifteen and only a few people were in the news-room, so I continued. I grabbed a new legal pad, a pen-and-paper gal when the notes were important. If I took them on the computer, I printed them immediately and marked them up in colors, noting what was slush, what was questionable, what might make the lede, what needed pursuit. I dialed the Sisters of St. Joseph, whose convent still existed nearby.

Sister Ellen answered the phone. "Good morning, Christ is Lord."

I hadn't confirmed that St. Joseph's was, in fact, the hospital, but I went with the strong hunch and told Sister Ellen the story.

"Bless you, dear child."

"Can you help?"

"What is it that you want?"

"I'm wondering if there are medical records for the infant."

Sister Ellen directed me to the Diocese of Brooklyn, which over-saw the Sisters and the hospital. As layered an operation as the Pentagon, the governing body for the area's parishes seemed impene-trable. My initial calls were ignored, and I sensed that this spoke of the research would take time and persistence. But it had been a productive morning so far, and I felt that whatever I ultimately learned about the baby's death would be helpful in some way. I had to remind myself that I wasn't reporting a story for publication but trying to understand my family.

"Got something for you," my assignment editor said, tapping on my desk. As a features writer, I had developed a reputation for finding odd and unexpected angles to stories that would, at first blush, seem straightforward. "You like cupcakes?"

"Chocolate."

"Perfect. Get your pen."

It seemed that two local guys, previously involved in a real estate operation that scammed hundreds of home sellers, had opened a cupcake bakery in the heart of downtown. Tom, my editor, figured that if these people were running the business, something untoward had to have been going on.

"Just go see," he said. "I've got nothing, but cheaters cheat."

"Scammers scam."

"Exactly."

I took off for Carolina Cakes. It wasn't Watergate, but there would be snacks.

In the car, I turned on the news, but my head was so full of facts and theories and dates, not to mention potential cupcake capers, that it couldn't take in any additional information. I flipped the station to Raleigh's best Top 40 and for fifteen minutes, I let my neocortex work its magic, absorbing and cataloging the data.

One person worked behind the counter at the bakery. It was a typical storefront set-up, with pink cafe tables and chairs and striped aqua walls. Magenta neon spelled out the company name in loopy script. I perused the case, counting four trays, one flavor on each, eight to ten cupcakes per tray, only thirty-five in total. They were average size, nothing like the mammoth trendsetter of the class, The Sparkles Cake, which had made its way east from Los Angeles two years earlier, eliciting block-long lines and a five-dollar price tag. Carolina's were not particularly inspiring…no swirls of frosting, no luscious colors, no cocoa shards or sugar sprinkles. Most interestingly, the shop was missing the bakery essence, the distinctive and instant and singular wallop: the aroma of cake in the oven.

"What's your best seller?"

"I don't really know." The woman looked bored behind the counter. "Maybe the red velvet."

"I'll try the Devil's Food, and a tea. Hot tea." I had learned to be specific in the south. "Do you bake here, if you don't mind my asking?"

She nodded no, smirking. "They bring them in."

"That's weird."

"Tell me."

I was the only customer in the store. "You here alone?"

I revealed my intended purpose, and for the next half hour, Taylor Tompkins, Carolina Cakes' Senior Sales Associate, vented. She hadn't yet been paid for her month of employment. Two co-workers had quit. The owners, who were generally absent, knew nothing about food, or even retail. Customers were sparse.

"I think they buy them from the supermarket," she said, half-serious.

She let me peek into the back room, where there were racks and cabinets, but no kitchen equipment of any kind.

"Was this space a boutique?"

"Shoe store."

"I knew it felt familiar. Bought patent leather boots here. Love them."

Before leaving the newsroom, I had looked up addresses for the owners. One lived in a duplex not far from the store. I drove to the house, a well-maintained Victorian the color of, dare I say, lemon. Seeing no suspicious activity, no pretend pastry chefs loading toques of cash into delivery trucks, I circled behind to the alley. The trash hadn't been picked up, fortunately, so I parked near the bins and got out, leaving the car idling and driver's door open. If only I had my batter-proof vest, alas. Checking both coasts, I lifted the lid.

Sometimes, the journalistic gods are feeling generous and shake presents down from the clouds, like gold dust. Sometimes, they bestow simple, undeniable gifts that land just when you need a stroke of good fortune. Just when you need to say, Had I left ten minutes later, I would have been hit by the eighteen-wheeler. Had I not been so thorough, so conscientious, I would not have found an envelope containing six receipts from Food Lion, each one listing fifteen identical items, fifteen testaments to fraud and deception, fifteen smoking ovens, as it were. Fifteen boxes of Betty Crocker cupcake mix. Times six.

I stashed the stash of receipts in my pocket, alley trash included in the public record and legally permissible in an investigation, and poked around with a stick for other evidence of foul play, not that ninety boxes of pre-fab cake mix weren't enough. Perhaps I'd solidify my case with unpaid invoices, letters from landlords, canned frosting.

A car honked, and I jumped back from the bin. A man wanted to get through. He sneered and shook his head. I dropped the stick, pulled the car door shut and headed back to the newsroom, victorious.

———————

Rox's ballet school took up the ground floor of a retail building in downtown Raleigh. She walked inside, her bag slung over her shoulder like a teenager, and I followed. In the dressing room, moms helped their daughters into their tights and leotards, if they hadn't put them on at home. Rox was lucky; she got to wear pink tights, despite her teensy age. She held both of my shoulders and raised one knee at a time, pointing each foot into its gathered leg. I unfurled them in my hands, the fabric rolling up her baby limbs. When it reached her waist, I lifted her up by the band and she rose an inch off the floor, giggling, thinking she had reached the ceiling. Or the moon.

During the hour, I waited in the reception area outside the studio, using the time to continue the day's work.

Another mom sat on the bench. "You must have been a dancer."

I looked up from where I was on the floor.

"From how you're sitting." She smiled.

One of my legs was stretched to the side, its foot flexed. The other was bent. Both hips were flat on the tile. A basic stretch.

"Look at me, I didn't even realize."

"Well, you've got the ballet body. I'm just a blubbery mess after those babies."

"You look great, just keep moving, that's the trick."

I called into my office phone to check for messages. "Miss Nichols, it's Susan Moore from St. John's. The name you were looking for is Sister Genevieve Paul. I'm hoping that helps."

I quickly called her back.

"Was this her name at birth?"

"That, I can't say. It's all that was written on the photograph."

I called Sister Ellen at the convent and provided the information. "It's true that most take the name of a saint, or two saints, as Sister Genevieve did. But we should have something in our archives.

We've been around for a hundred and fifty years, you know."

"Quite a history, and you've done so much good work."

"Thank you, dear. I will find the name."

That anything would come of Sister Genevieve Paul's presence in the photo was questionable, but good reporters follow all leads until they're dry. Until they're shaken like a rug in the spring. Hollowed out. Raked.

Roxy flew out of the studio after class and flopped next to me on the floor. "We did piqués, Mommy. Like the letters. P and K. Look." She stood back up and showed me.

"Those are beautiful, Rox. Did you have fun?"

"Lots."

She traded her slippers for her sneaks, and we headed for home.

"Put on JT, Mommy."

I pressed the button and the CD started. *Shower the people you love with love...*

In the mirror, I watched her sing along, strapped in and safe. I had worried about being a mother on my own, not about the day-to-day logistics, but about giving Roxy everything that I thought she would need to feel secure. Would I be present when she needed something explained, when she fell off a bike, when she didn't know what to do? Would I say the right thing? Would I make it better? Just a month in, I had already witnessed her distress and felt help-less. I worried, continually, about what other hurdles would get in her way as she grew up.

Each Sunday since her birth, we cooked a special dinner, a ritual that I had continued after the divorce. We set the table with a cloth and used Grandma Lilly's china. The night before, after the first week-end at Jeff's house, I didn't plan for the meal, thinking that Roxy would need to settle back in quietly and go to sleep early. Listening to her sing in the car, I determined not to miss another Sunday, as the custom was important for both of us, perhaps more than it had been before.

Beginning the next weekend, we stirred and baked and put flowers in a vase. We sat at the table and talked and laughed and planned. And I looked at my daughter and took stock, privately, having the conversation with myself. Is she growing well? Does she feel happy with herself? Am I doing a good job, no, am I doing the best job? The very best job?

Then, I would tell myself to keep that pang in my ribs in check, that yes, there has been some strain but there is beauty that will emerge from it, from the impediments, from even the terrifying knowledge that I might fail her. No single mother wants to fail her child—provide less, teach less, support less, be less—but it was in my mind that I might. Already, I sensed the struggle. I would need to impart to Roxy that trials can be good. She would know this intimately, and it would serve her well.

I pulled into the driveway, and we went inside. Sister Ellen had left another message: Sister Genevieve Paul was born in 1903 as Mary Lynn McDermott. She worked at the hospital from 1933 until 1956 and would have lived at the convent and likely never married or had children before becoming a nun.

Of course, she could have had McDermott brothers who had other McDermotts, and other McDermotts, but this, I feared, was a reporting rabbit hole. I put Sister Genevieve Paul on hold, as much as I was intrigued. Confirmation would have to come another way.

THIRTY

Two weeks later, an envelope from New York arrived in my mailbox.

When I spoke with the Records Commissioner, I told him that a baby had died, and that it may have been an accident, and that I was the niece. It was odd saying "niece."

I hurried inside the house, dropping the rest of the mail onto the foyer table. Not knowing what it contained, I eased the edge of the envelope open and unfolded the paper inside, black and white, a copy of the original.

Across the top, it read, "Certificate of Death."

In words attesting to his demise, the baby suddenly came to life.

In capitals on the first line, the initial details were confirmed.

"Place of Death: Borough of Queens"

Underneath, the specific location.

"Institution: St. Joseph Hospital of Far Rockaway"

My stomach jumped. I drew in a breath. Sister Genevieve and Mary Lynn McDermott and all of the McDermotts smacked around in my head, wearing nuns' habits and hospital uniforms and suits and wing-tips, filling up the nursery, jostling around the bassinets, a swarm.

On the next line, there was a space for the person's name. I was expecting it to be blank.

"Full Name: Abraham Goldman"

I dropped back onto the wall and closed my eyes.

Abraham. He had been named, after all, and for Grandma Lilly's dad, who had died a year before her wedding. My mom had spoken his name so many times. Ben had written its iteration, Albert, near-ly every day, spelling out his middle name on school papers and in his signature. My grandmother's choice seemed obvious.

I sensed there was more to come. Eager, at first, to learn the facts as I would any facts to any story, I was now hesitant, fearful, like the next of kin in the waiting room. I felt connected to the baby as I hadn't before. I felt his loss.

"Date of Birth: October 2, 1932"

"Date of Death: October 6, 1932, 10:30 AM"

"Age: 4 days"

The image of the cart flashed, its low sides, its cold metal. Then, Grandma Lilly, hysterical, by the nursery window, her auburn hair quivering over her face. She would have gone to the window. She would have screamed in horror. She would have flung her arms and smacked the glass and buckled over, pain seething where birth and hope and joy had ripped her body open.

I sat down and read further. During the week before the document arrived, I played out the scenarios. If there was a specific description of a cause of death, one that indicated an accident, the hospital could have been culpable. If a different reason was given, the hospital could have been guilty of altering the truth. There would be nothing, I was convinced. The space would have been empty. No one from the state would have questioned the hospital's omission in 1932, the charita-ble Catholic hospital's omission, if it was even noticed.

But in the right column, about halfway down, a Dr. William Johnson had written something in script. A capital "H." A loopy "t." The details, unbelievably. And finally.

"Hemorrhage into brain, skin, testicles"

I sat on the foyer bench, imagining a tiny body with blotches of blood beneath its surface, spreading as the seconds passed, consum-ing it. Turning the pearly white to red. Is it red? Claret? Aubergine?

While Dr. William Johnson didn't write in fanciful cursive what spurred the hemorrhage into the brain, it is commonly understood that trauma is often the impetus, trauma from head injury, specifi-cally. Abraham must have hit the rest on the way down.

I suppose that Dr. William Johnson could feel good, or less guilty, or quite sly that he at least wrote something. He, accurately, I suspect, described the medical reason for Abraham's death, but he didn't report how the medical reason came about. Hemorrhage into brain, skin, testicles *due to* what. A rare condition that affects healthy symptom-free newborns four days after birth? An accident? A crime? Such different sets of emotions would attach to each possibility. Without knowing which it was, whether by choice or failure to know how to find out, my grandparents had to contend with the feelings wrought by all of them. A tidal wave.

I picked up the paper and read on. At the bottom of the page, a cemetery was listed, as well as the date of interment. Uncle Abraham, who died at 10:30 on the morning of October 6, was also buried on October 6.

No one is buried on the same day.

THIRTY-ONE

OVER THE PHONE, THE man at Acadia Cemetery in Elmont, New York said that Uncle Abraham is buried in Section F, Block 3, Row D, Grave 4. He had no documentation for who arranged for and brought the body exactly seventy years earlier, who was present for the interment, or who paid for the services. He could not tell me if the delivery person appeared distracted or if his hands shook or if he skidded away quickly. Or if he made himself known, even, or said too much or too little.

The man at Acadia Cemetery could not tell me whether the baby was dressed in bunny pajamas or swaddled in a blanket, whether he arrived having been transported in a brown box from the hospital supply room or a soup tureen from the kitchen, having skipped a proper visit to the funeral home. A proper visit for prettying up and making comfortable, for erasing the signs that led him there to begin with, for making him look nice for the living the one last time. So, did Baby Goldman arrive stashed in a canvas sack or laid out in a surgical tray? Or did St. Joseph's have a casket stored in some remote closet, just in case? A wee infant casket, with silky white satin lining the inside?

———————

"Has the plot been kept up?" I asked the man over the phone.

His voice was somber. "There has been no care."

"Ever?"

"Not ever."

THIRTY-TWO

BEN HAD BECOME AN orthopedic surgeon and lived in New York. He was married to a woman he met on a walk through Central Park. While watching the model boat races in Conservatory Water, he noticed her sitting on the bench next to his. She had a favorite that day, a hand-made wooden yacht with a blue-striped sail.

He called to her, the story goes, and asked which was the one she liked.

"The schooner. My neighbor makes them in his apartment. That's him, with the fishing hat."

Ben would not have another Saturday off from the hospital, where he was chief resident, for the next six weeks. He asked if he could join her on her bench, where they talked until the racing concluded two hours later. Alice's neighbor competed well, coming in third.

They married a year and a half later and took photos by the pond. Edward Thompson III, the schooner-designer and art historian/ mentor/best friend, toasted the couple at the wedding, an intimate gathering for seventy-five at a downtown loft. He claimed responsibility for their chance meeting, using sea-faring terminology like *ballast* and *bearing*. Alice, an architect with exquisite taste, Rapunzel hair and delicate limbs, sewed her own veil, incorporating satin buds from the wedding dress that her mother wore.

I called Ben to ask him about hemorrhaging. Could it have been caused, in this case, by something other than a fall, I wondered. Ben was my personal repository of medical knowledge. I had consulted him on numerous stories as well as issues with Roxy. Fortunately, none were more serious than inflamed bug bites or ear infections.

"In infants, there's Vitamin K deficiency, which can cause bleeding. The vitamin's a clotting factor, and now, we just give the babies injections at birth. What's this story about?"

"I'm researching Mom's dead brother. Finally."

"Really. Haven't thought of that in a long time."

"I know, it's been a while." I thought about his answer. "They wouldn't have had injections in 1932, would they? And would the bleeding look the same as something traumatic?"

"Tell me again what the death certificate says, exactly."

I spoke the words into the phone.

"I doubt they had injections then…you can look that up easily. And talk with an O-B…it's been a while since med school, but I think the bleeding is in the brain and internally. The testicles sound inconsistent."

"He was buried the same day."

"It says that? Wow. No one is buried the same day."

"Exactly."

"And there were rumors about a fall, right?"

"According to Mom."

"Circumstantial, but someone probably heard something to start a rumor. Could be Vitamin K, but could be trauma. Either way, it's pretty horrendous."

"So I should check out what causes testicular hemorrhaging."

"In newborns. What else is going on? How's Rox?"

"The best. She's reading lots of words, and she loves the ballet."

"Of course she does."

In the days that followed, I was preoccupied with Abraham. I thought about his time in the hospital and also what had been waiting for him at home. The salt air on the boardwalk, his grandmother Beatrice's cabbage soup. Show tunes rising from the Spinet, a tidier version of the upright piano, invented in the decade of his birth. Papa Sam had the latest inside the Goldman household. I felt sad those days, heartbroken, really, and not just for my grandparents, but for the first time, for all of us. Seventy years later, I felt grief.

I realized that Lilly's profound sorrow had to have been reawakened each time she faced a loss. Like Abraham, her despair was buried out of sight, sublimated, abandoned. With each successive separation, it surfaced, unaddressed, only to be squelched again, the anguish building incrementally.

After giving birth, she suffered excessive pain during every menstrual cycle. My mother said that it was visible, sending her to lie down, to crunch up in bed. The pathos of it, the symbolism, is almost too contrived. The enduring reminder. The endless assault. So, I cannot believe that my grandmother subdued the trauma such that it evacuated her body and brain, that she was able to trick herself, to make frilly hats and wear beautiful dresses and sing and play piano. I believe that she tried, desperately, by herself, to do so but was beaten each time. Outsmarted. And with each defeat, I believe that she hurt alone.

When my mom married and left home for good, Lilly must have been distraught, the mother-child bond between them so deep. When we moved farther away, even if only an hour's distance, she must have felt the slip, the imminent disappearance. Ultimately, when she and Sam left for Florida, the umbilical cord was severed definitively. Lilly was untethered. She was retraumatized. She called us on the phone and said that she was going to die.

It was then, two generations later, that she finally faced her grief. It was then that she mourned her baby boy.

Vitamin K was discovered in 1927 but wasn't understood to be a clotting factor until 1935. The lack of it at birth was not associated with *hemorrhagic disease of the newborn* until 1939, though the condition had been reported since the 17th century, with many different reasons besides trauma given for its occurrence. Typically, an afflicted infant may present with intrathoracic or intra-abdominal bleeding, which can be seen on x-ray. He may also bleed from the umbilical stump, the mucous membranes or the skin. Intracranial bleeding, which Abraham had, is mostly associated with late emergence of the condition, after two weeks.

Of the three body parts mentioned on Abraham's death certificate—brain, testicles and skin—only the last is consistent with early hemorrhagic disease in newborns, occurring within the first week. Brain bleeding is rare for a four-day-old, and testicular hemorrhage is not specified in the research.

When Abraham was born in 1932, doctors would not have been aware that natural Vitamin K deficiency in babies could cause internal bleeding, but they would have been accustomed to their dying from it, particularly in a hospital in a big city. The infant mortality rate in the United States that year was fifty-eight out of a thousand births. In Queens County, it was forty-three. Some research suggests that one of two hundred babies experienced hemorrhaging within the first week after birth. The treatment, then, as for internal bleeding due to any number of causes, would have been transfusion, as Papa Sam had given.

Eleven babies, including Abraham, were buried at Acadia Cemetery in 1932. Four were boys. Two of their death certificates listed hemorrhage as the cause of death; neither mentioned the testicles.

While Abraham could have been a medical exception, developing intracranial bleeding earlier than most and testicular bleeding when others hadn't, the hospital's behaviors surrounding his death didn't seem consistent with something they had seen before. Presuming that his condition wasn't the hospital's first, they would have had to relay the news to parents before. They would have had to tell them something. Not all would have had to press for answers, for weeks. Not all would have sent nurses running away from them in town. Not all would have buried their babies within hours of their deaths.

Of the eleven Acadia infants, only Abraham suffered such a fate.

Successive interviews with Carolina Cupcakes employees revealed a trail of broken contracts, threats and complaints. The landlord of the retail property reported late rent payments but had made accommodations with their tenants, Trevor and Mike. The landlord of the yellow Victorian, where Trevor and Mike lived, was not as patient.

"I'm going over there the end of the week, if you want to come. They owe me for two months."

Trevor and Mike had agreed to my request for an interview but stood me up, so I gladly accepted the offer. This little story was turning out to be a fun one; alley trash and now an ambush.

While searching for a pair of earrings that morning, I came across my grandmother's locket. I put it on and wore it every day after.

Later, I parked down the street from the house and met Tim, the landlord, on the sidewalk.

"Their cars aren't here," I said.

"We'll knock once and then go in. I have the key."

Through the porch window, I could see that the apartment was empty, except for a couch. The Cupcake Kings had decamped.

Inside, I went straight to the kitchen and opened the cabinets. "Sorry about the rent money."

"It happens. Take your time, I'm going to check for damage."

The shelves over the counter were all empty. Underneath, I found a couple of pots and frying pans before making my way to the oven. I yanked open the door, anticipating what waited on the other side. These fake bakers were neither careful nor intelligent. They would not have disposed of the evidence in Sand Rock Lake, heaving their brick-weighted twelve-holed non-stick tins into the swirly depths. They would have left them, all fourteen of them, stacked where the deed was done, drips of Devil's Food burnt onto their rims.

In the pantry were seventy-seven unused boxes of the Betty Crocker mix. They had used thirteen of them since purchasing them four days earlier, according to the receipts. I took print-worthy photos of my findings and cataloged the cupcake flavors to cross-reference with what the store sold in the prior days. No circumstantial evidence allowed, thank you very much.

"Got what you need?" Tim asked.

186

"A bonanza. How are the other rooms?"

"Cleared out. I don't know how they do it, screw you and keep going, without looking back."

"There are people like that," I said.

"They'll implode, they always do. Maybe fifty years from now, but it'll get 'em. Boom."

Driving back to the office, I kept hearing Tim's words...*Boom. Fifty years from now, Boom.* He had lifted his hands up and slapped them together when he said it. The sound rang out in the vacant apartment.

I took the elevator up to the newsroom. Tim's remark sent me straight to Florida, visiting Grandma Lilly in her nightgown at two in the afternoon, hearing her whimper about her demise. If this was imploding, then it was gradual. It wasn't a *Boom.*

One of the statehouse reporters hopped on before the doors shut. "What's the word?" he said, catching his breath, interrupting my thoughts. Jason Tierney always asked this. It was a cumbersome question to answer, grammatically, without getting into a comprehensive explanation of the thing he wanted to know. You couldn't say *Not much* or *Pretty good*, throw-away responses to standard inquiries from work acquaintances thrust into your physical space. Those phrases wouldn't make sense.

But Jason Tierney had twinkly eyes and well-worn Oxford button-downs, so his question wasn't as annoying to me as it could have been.

"Cupcakes," I said. "The word is cupcakes."

"High crimes and misdemeanors."

"You mock, but you'll see."

The door opened, and he followed me out. "Well, go to it," he said, turning left, trotting off. Jason Tierney rarely walked.

Normally, I would have formulated the lede to the story by this point, wanting to sit down and start writing as soon as I hit my desk. Instead, I dropped my bag on the chair and continued around the perimeter of the room, down a hallway, through the reception area and back into the newsroom from the other side. I was addled and itchy. Thoughts careened in my head, none of them catching. I picked up the pace, my body wanting to shake out the nagging, recalibrate.

"Hey. Cupcake. You're going to wear out the carpet," Jason Tierney said as I passed his desk.

I stopped and turned around. Sun shot in from the windows and lit up the blond in his hair.

"You okay?" he asked. "You look spooked or something."

I took off for the bathroom, suddenly feeling sick. I bent over the sink, splashing water on my face, shaking. The faucet ran, and I held on to the counter, trying to slow my breaths, calm the panic in my chest.

When my grandfather went to the hospital and Grandma Lilly failed to take her insulin, we believed that she was worried and confused. She was out of sorts, her routine having been disrupted. Her death, we thought, was preventable. Papa Sam was the man who cushioned her, protected her, carried her through, and he had left, if only temporarily. But Lilly could see this just one way, the way that she was conditioned to see it when people left. The people she loved went away, and they didn't return. Sam was next in line, and she couldn't bear such loss again. She couldn't repress such loss again.

Water dripped down my face, mixing with tears. My grandmother intended to ignore her medication that day, fully aware of the consequences. The tragedy was not that it was an oversight. It was that she chose to go.

It'll get 'em. Boom.

THIRTY-THREE

A FEW DAYS LATER, the 1940 Census reports for Lilly, Sam and my great-grandparents arrived in the mail.

The Goldmans had two children, the document confirmed in the second column, Abraham and Eva. The two names were listed, one under the other, as if they shared a household, built drippy sand castles, played Parcheesi in their pajamas. They were a family of four, in the second column, a boy and a girl perfectly spaced and two parents. Ideal. They would grow up together, the boy and the girl, contemporaries always. They'd giggle in the back seat of the car. They'd introduce each other to their friends. They'd be as close as people could be.

For as long as I could divert my eyes, I didn't look at the third column.

When someone asked, my mother described herself as an only child. She lived with the status, never having known a sibling, seen one sleeping in another bed, eating dinner in another chair. But a person existed, if only briefly, a person who lived and breathed and cried, who clung to the same breast, smelled the same scent, belonged in the same place. When someone asked, then, was she to say, "Yes, I am an only child, now, anyway, and for all of my days, though I had a brother who died before I was born, I think, maybe... but no one said." Was she to say that? Must she have said that?

Lilly's parents settled in Brooklyn and had four children, I had believed. There was Horace, then Frannie, Edward and finally Lilly. But the census listed another child, a fifth born to Abraham and Beatrice, a son tucked in between my grandmother and Edward. There

189

was a Charles, born on Valentine's Day in 1898.

I scoured my work computer, which had access to databases that I didn't have at home. I found a draft card for World War I. At twenty, Charles was called to the Army. He had brown hair and eyes and a medium build, and he was a clerk at H. Rosinsky & Co., his older brother's clothing company at 107 East 17th Street. On September 12, 1918, just two months before the war was to end, he left his home on Ocean Avenue in Brooklyn, near Prospect Park, and did not return. He went by Charlie.

Lilly was just fourteen when he was sent away. His death was her first loss. A sibling close in age. Children, both. Lilly buried him deep inside of her, never mentioning him to my mom or me, establishing the pattern of silent suffering that she would never shake.

Like a floral repeat in a calico print, or a chevron, clover or chain, the practice of smothering grief was entrenched in my mother's family. The consequences were traumatic for Grandma Lilly. My mother could do it handily, though; muffling the uncomfortable or the outright sad seemed a cinch.

I wondered how I came to think about Abraham when I did, how feelings stashed away since childhood became conscious to me, such that I needed to act. As a child, I couldn't recognize or understand this unspoken legacy, though I felt it, rubbing the wrong way, sitting off-center. Wobbling, without ever coming to a stop.

It made sense that I would think about him the first time Roxy went off on her own, without me.

THIRTY-FOUR

ROXY WAS INVITED TO a dress-up birthday party and decided to be Henry's best friend, a corgi from across the street. The costume-making process was in full swing when my mother arrived from New York for a week-long visit, the dining table strewn with caramel-colored fleece and pipe-cleaner whiskers, curved and cut to size. She came to Raleigh about three times a year after Roxy was born and stayed with us in the spare bedroom. This was her first trip following my divorce, and I was looking forward to having some help at home, if only for a few days.

"Maybe you need to be done with this, this separation," she said, within an hour of landing. "Okay, so, he slept with someone. Men can't control themselves. It's not big news."

"It's big to me."

"Well, you should get over that."

I felt the tightening of the muscle at the top of my stomach, the internal intercostal. This one particular chord of tissue contracted when my mother imposed her judgment, a warning to the rest of my anatomy. Such statements weren't surprising, but they were hard to fend off. Before you knew it, you had become entangled in a back-and-forth about a subject you had no interest in exploring, or exploring with her. The only way to avoid an engagement was to leave, physically, or remain silent, which only ignited additional tension. My strategy was to answer succinctly and shift topics.

"For the ears, I was thinking of making a headband rather than a hood," I said. "What do you think?"

"No hood, it's too hot. So muggy here. Dreadful."

The idea of being alone without a man was anathema to my mother. Immediately after my dad died, she began dating. His death angered her more than it caused grief, or simple sadness, even. She seemed put upon by the notion of his absence and what it meant for her daily and future existence, her plans, her finances, her calendar. She did not collapse in any sort of sorrow. She did not emerge from her bedroom, puffy-eyed and forlorn. She did not take care of her devastated children.

At the time, her reaction was astounding to me, hurtful and diminishing. I knew from childhood that she was not the most compassionate parent, but I wasn't prepared for the kind of self-absorption that she exhibited when my father died. But now, her response made sense. Pain and heartache were not allowed, uncomfortable as they were, even if it meant consoling her children. Eva Nichols was not going to be made uncomfortable.

"Have fun always," she wrote on a birthday card just months after the burial, never having said that she was sorry my father was gone, that he'd miss two-thirds of my life.

The words became her personal mantra. Living it, she went out with men, one after the other. And, she thought it appropriate to share her escapades with Ben and me, to relay details about Roger's preference for opera or Bill's sports car or Rick's penis, persisting despite our objections. For nearly a year, I didn't answer the phone when she called. A man I didn't know left me a message, saying my mother's feelings were hurt.

"Eva is very upset," he said. "You should talk to her." The presumption was as offensive as her behavior.

I didn't excuse it or apologize for avoiding it. It felt as if I had lost two parents at once.

That night, Roxy showed her grandmother her ballet steps, insisting on taking off her pajamas and putting on her leotard, tights and slippers. I played a Minuet on the piano, and my mom watched from the sofa, applauding after every leap and grand battement. Afterward, I cleaned up the kitchen and Mom supervised the teeth-brushing and story-reading before bed. It felt downright luxurious washing the dishes without juggling the other responsibilities.

———————

Late the next afternoon, my mother came downstairs in a black catsuit.

"Grandma's wearing a leotard," Roxy said.

She held a copy of Raleigh Magazine, folded open to the ads at the back. Her eyes were ringed with liner, lips painted in deep plum. Shalimar puffed from her perimeter, like steam from a pot.

Roxy sniffed her thigh. "She smells good, Mommy."

I set up paper, markers and crayons on the little table in the den. A moth to the light.

"Here, Katie, can you do the clasp for me?" my mother asked, raising a chain in her hand.

"Are you serious?"

"Of course I'm serious."

I left the room for the kitchen. Her heels clicked behind me.

"What are you here for?" I spun around and looked into her painted face. "Don't you have enough men to go out with in New York? You have to have them here, too?"

She put on her own necklace and checked it in the hall mirror.

"It's just beyond imagination, the disrespect," I called to her, hearing my voice crescendo. "One day, and it's too much for you to help me sew a costume, watch a movie with your granddaughter. Too much."

"I told you not to go through with it, the divorce."

"That's your answer. You blame me," I yelled. "I can't take this."

"Don't, then." She turned upside down and fluffed her hair.

"How do you do it? You had a husband you didn't mourn. You had a mother begging for help your entire life and a brother who fell off a goddam hospital cart. And you just step over the carnage."

"What are you hollering about? My mother...what does she have to do with anything?"

"How do you pretend these horrible things don't happen? How do you not realize that bad things affect other people? Affect me? You strut around in jeans, telling me how good they look because you lost weight, when my father is upstairs on oxygen, dying. You tell me about a dead baby when I'm eight and that you slept with men a month after Dad's buried in the ground. Then you bring them to my house for lunch. For lunch! And you think it's all okay. I'm supposed to make chicken salad. Who told you it was all okay?"

I leaned on the kitchen table, crying, coughing from the outburst.

"What has gotten into you?" she said. "And you have no idea."

"Really? Did you know that you had another uncle? Charlie. Died in World War One when he was twenty. Did you know that? And guess what else, your poor mother killed herself. Skipped the insulin. On purpose. While you're sitting up in New York, being busy. How's that for an idea I don't know about."

My mother stared at me, motionless, the personal ads still rolled up in her hand. Suddenly, from beyond the kitchen, I heard rapid steps and a squeaky hinge and the whoosh of Carolina wind. A streak of black and white—Henry—tore past. Instantly, I knew that Roxy had run outside. The arguing had scared her, and she took off. I screamed to her, calling her name, yelling for her to stop, racing down the hallway toward the foyer, where the door flapped open and shut, a valve in the heart, misfiring.

We lived on a narrow street that allowed parking on both sides, leaving room for one car to pass through in between. People used the street to get to and from the elementary school, a couple of blocks away. Sometimes they drove too fast.

I crossed the threshold and leaped down the porch steps, seeing a flash to my right, a young, agile, speedy flash of a daughter, sprinting toward the street. A car swerved around the corner, two houses down. My shrieks rang dull in my head, the way you can't flee in a dream or rise up from drowning. Never run into the road, I told her, since she was a baby, since before she could speak or comprehend or crawl. Never run into the road after anything, I told her, swaddled up in her bassinet, belted in her stroller, clasped in my arms. Remember what I taught you, I yelled in my head. Now, this instant, remember it, remember everything. Roxy, I called, but the voice couldn't come. My arms couldn't reach. My legs wouldn't move. A blur, a ponytail, a sneaker, obscured by the white oak, absent from view. Skids of tires. Mayhem in my gut.

I careened around the tree and collapsed to the ground. Roxy lay on her side in the bed of hydrangeas, wailing, holding her leg. She had tripped on the root of the oak that protruded from the path, smacking the stone wall along the way, saved from the street. I feared that she had hit her head or twisted her spine, and I was afraid to move her, holding her in place with my arms and body, her cries and trembles mingling with mine.

"You're okay, you're okay," I whispered, pressing my hands into every inch of her, checking for pain. "What hurts, what hurts?"

She sat up on her own and clung to me. Her leg was bruised and her ankle already swollen. She had cuts on her face and arms and hands. Blood dripped toward her eye.

"Henry," she cried. "Where's Henry?"

"You're okay, oh God, you're okay."

I looked up and saw that the oncoming car had stopped in the street, its wheels pointing into the curb. A man approached from the far side of the road, carrying our little pet in his arms. As he got closer, I saw Henry's one ear perk up.

"He's perfectly fine," said the man, bending down. "Was talking to his buddy across the street. Here, let me help you."

I scooped Roxy up and hurried toward the path, where my mother was standing. I blew past her and called out to the man, or my mother, or no one, hearing my voice quiver, feeling my bones shake. "I'm going to get some ice. Ice, Roxy, ice."

The man stood on the path, holding Henry.

I put Roxy on the couch, elevating her leg and checking every centimeter under her clothing for injuries. My mother filled a dish towel with ice cubes and brought it to me.

"Gauze, under my bathroom sink," I said.

The man came inside and placed Henry on the floor. "I'm going to move my car."

Roxy's ankle had doubled in size in the few minutes that had passed. She wiped the blood on her forehead and squealed when she saw it on her hand.

My mother brought the gauze and went outside. It occurred to me that the man was her date.

THIRTY-FIVE

ACCURATE X-RAYS ARE DIFFICULT to achieve if the tissue is too swollen. I iced Roxy's ankle for an hour—on for ten, off for ten—before taking her to the emergency room. She couldn't bear weight, and I was concerned that she may have fractured the tibia. I put clean gauze on her forehead and taped it down with Band-Aids. Then I carried her to the car, sat her sideways in the back seat and drove to the hospital.

I looked at her in the rearview mirror. "How does your head feel?"

She touched the side of it.

"Inside, does it hurt inside? Or feel funny?"

She nodded no. "Just my foot."

"Are you dizzy?"

"Just my foot."

"But you're not faint?"

"What's faint?"

I didn't know if Roxy remembered why she ran outside or if the fright of her fall eradicated what preceded it. I wanted to tell her I was sorry for yelling, ravaged with guilt for yelling, petrified to my core for yelling, but I didn't want to risk reminding her right then. That conversation would wait, and I would live with the anguish, meantime, and likely forever. All I could see was her little body sprawled in the street.

The doctor determined that she did not suffer a concussion, but the cut near her hairline would need three stitches.

"Baby skin heals so well, you'll never know," he said.

Her tibia was intact, as was the more delicate fibula, or so it seemed for now. She had a severe sprain and bone bruise, though, which could take some time to heal. She left the E-R with her ankle splinted and wrapped and orders to return in two days for another x-ray. From drawing with crayons at the little table in the den to this, in seconds.

A nursing assistant wheeled Roxy out to the car and strapped her into the back seat. "You're a brave girl."

It had gotten dark, and the house was lit up when we pulled into the driveway. I ducked into the back seat and lifted Roxy out. She held onto my neck with both arms, worn out. The front door opened as I trudged up the path.

I stepped past my mother and carried Roxy upstairs to her bed. The house smelled like soup and braised chicken. From the bathroom, I got a basin and a towel and washed her hands and face, dabbing her bruised skin and patting it dry. My mother came quietly into the room, handed me a pair of pajamas and scooped up the dirty clothes, the towel and container of soapy water. She had changed out of her catsuit.

"Do you feel like eating?" I asked Roxy.

She nodded.

"I made minestrone," my mother said from the doorway.

"How about some soup?" I asked.

"And chicken, too," Roxy said. "It smells like chicken."

We set up a picnic on a small table in her bedroom, emblazoned with unicorns whirling on a carousel. Rox sat on the tiny chair, her leg propped on a stack of pillows. Not too much later, she took pain medication and fell asleep. I pulled the cushions off the den sofa and put them on the floor by her bed, with a blanket and pillow, where I would sleep.

I found my mother in the living room. "I'm going to take a shower and go to bed. Jeff is coming by the house tomorrow after work. I'll be staying home, and Roxy will skip school."

"That all sounds good."

"Turn out the lights, except for the one in the corner."

She sat with her hands folded on her lap, looking as if she wanted to speak.

"Thank you for making dinner," I said and left the room.

THIRTY-SIX

THE NEXT DAY, ROXY scooted on her rear end down the steps to the kitchen, where my mother had covered the table in newspaper and set up paints and brushes.

"You go do what you need to do," she said, waving me off.

I didn't know what to expect from her. She ignored problems and simply carried on as if nothing had happened. But this was different. She loved her granddaughter, and the near miss had to have rattled her.

In the afternoon, as soon as Roxy laid down for a nap, my mother appeared next to my desk, where I had gone to try to work. I put down my pen.

She sat, sliding back in Dad's captain's chair, a gift from his residency program. I kept it next to my desk. "The baby wasn't part of my life," she said, carefully. "I was too young to understand, and I wasn't inquisitive, like you. No one mentioned it after a while, and it disappeared."

"For you, but not for Grandma."

"Look, I feel bad for my mom to go through that. She catered to me because of it. So I couldn't pick at her, asking questions. I was her only child."

By hiding the story from her daughter, my grandmother had protected her from contending with it, from ever feeling guilty, from having to compensate for the baby who was lost. Grandma Lilly had succeeded, to a fault.

"But you weren't her only child. Don't you feel anything for him?"

She shrugged her shoulders, unaffected. "To me, it wasn't a him."

"His name was Abraham. He was born three years before you on October 2. He died on October 6, at St. Joseph's Hospital, and he was buried the same day."

"What? How do you know this?"

"I've been researching."

"Abraham? That's my mom's father. You know, she wore blue at her wedding because he had died." She took a beat. "Of course, Abraham."

"Why did you tell me this when I was eight? Did you know how scared I was?"

"I never would have told you then." She shifted in her seat. "And what did you mean yesterday when you said my mother killed herself? That is ridiculous, Kate. Really."

"Wait, you don't remember telling me?"

"Not when you were that little."

"Were you aware at the time?"

"Oh, god, I don't know. We didn't dwell so much back then, not like you mothers today."

Incredulous, I told her that I thought that Grandma Lilly failed to take her insulin on purpose, fearing that Papa Sam was the next person to abandon her. I was aware of everything that I told Roxy, when I said it, where, why, what shoes I had on.

"She wouldn't do that. She got to be a little scattered later in life, but she wouldn't do that."

I let her talk.

"I went all the time. We were best friends. My father doted on her. She had everything she could ever want. I didn't have a husband like that."

I bristled.

"Your father, he was never home. Sharon Brant went to the Bahamas, always in the city, out to restaurants. Those kids lived at our house." She looked disgusted. "I gave up a lot of fun to marry your father. So, I'm having fun now. You don't know."

"What don't I know?"

"He was difficult, and his family. Never thought I was good

enough, especially that Eleanor. How dare they."

"Lots of in-laws are like that."

"After what I did."

"You mean, be his wife? All married people do things for their spouses."

She stared at me, narrowing her eyes.

"What?" I said. "After you did what?"

She sat in my father's chair, her hands clasped under her chin, her head jiggling left and right. And then she shot up and smoothed down her sleeves. "You don't know the half of it."

"The half of what? That they didn't like you and he was so serious. Such crimes. Try having a husband who sleeps with someone else."

She swatted her hands and left the room.

THIRTY-SEVEN

LATER THAT EVENING, I overheard my mother talking on the phone in the spare room off the kitchen. Her voice was sweet-sounding and flirtatious.

"Well, it's no pleasure trip, but it's good I'm here."

"That sounds like fun."

"I'll be home soon, sweetie."

I stood outside the door and listened. Roxy was sleeping upstairs. My mother emerged from the room, smiling, giddy from the chat. She had mentioned one man more than the others, Stan. Maybe she had been talking with Stan.

"Ooh, you startled me," she said.

"Which one was that?"

"What do you mean? Stan, it was Stan. He wants to go to the Cape."

I looked for something to eat in the kitchen. "So, you have no problem cheating on Stan."

"Who's cheating?"

"You went on a date yesterday, or planned to, before his car nearly hit your granddaughter."

She stopped talking. "That's not cheating." Her mouth quivered. "And she's fine, thank God."

"No? What is it, then?" I grabbed a handful of pretzels from a bag.

"I don't owe anybody anything. I'm not married."

"It's sleazy. And disrespectful." I swallowed and took a drink of water. "Dad wouldn't have acted this way."

She slapped her hand on the counter. "Oh, for god's sake, Kate. Get off your high horse. And stop idolizing the man, already."

"The man?" I burned inside.

Part of me knew that she was jealous of my love for my father, whether she realized it or not. It didn't occur to me when I was younger whether my devotion to my dad would actually bother her, as boisterous and seemingly confident as she appeared. And, though I was pretty empathic as a kid, I was less so with my mother, more occupied with managing the emotional disquiet that she caused than understanding her feelings. I didn't really think of her as having sensitivities. If I had, maybe her behavior would have made better sense.

"He wouldn't run around with all sorts of women, whether I idolized him or not."

"Well, pardon me for living. And your perfect father?" She laughed. "He was no angel."

I figured she would tell me that he yelled when she lost her keys or wanted to leave early from parties. "I know, he was no fun, got testy. I know all about it."

She shook her head and paced. "You really don't."

"Okay, I know nothing. Fine. I'm so sick of this." I threw the bag of pretzels back into the cabinet. "It's really enough. I've just had it, with…"

"He had another kid." She bent over the counter. "Your perfect father."

Another grenade, dropped cavalierly from her manicured fist. "Right, Mom." I scoffed. "What is wrong with you?"

She looked at me as if I was the crazy one.

"Why would you say such a thing?"

"It's true."

"Jesus, Mom, I can't even respond to this, it's so unbelievable that you would verbalize something so insane. I'm going to bed. Jesus. This is your best one yet."

"Kate," she called as I reached the doorway. "I'm not making it up."

I turned around. Her eyebrows wrinkled. Her hand pressed a

cheek. She stared at me, saying nothing.

I steadied myself against the wall. "I would have known, if it was true. He would have told me."

"He told no one, not even me."

Chills rippled from my feet to my scalp. I was sticky and cold. Nauseated. Electrical currents tore through my flesh. My legs sucked down into the floor boards, into a vortex, stretching me, spinning me. The table was across the room. I held on to the counter and walked to a chair. My mother put a glass of water in front of me and sat down.

"What evidence do you have?" I said slowly, hearing my words sail the currents, distorted.

"A checkbook."

I sipped the water. It shook and spilled over the rim.

"When he was a freshman. A local girl, Irish Catholic family, with six kids and now a baby out of wedlock. He sent money every month, and he had none. He thought I'd never marry him, and it wouldn't look good for a doctor back then. I saw the checks."

I covered my mouth with my palms. My throat dried up, and the room spun. I couldn't breathe. The image of him that day that I pushed him to answer me, that fear in him, was vivid. Questions descended on me, like crows.

"He told you this?"

"I saw the checks, sitting there in the drawer. He couldn't hide it at that point."

"How long?"

"Since you and Ben were toddlers. And you think I'm not loyal."

I tried to make sense of the timeline, the motivation. The toll on my mother. On him. The half-sister. The shock of it consumed me. The confusion about who he was tangled me up. Was he the same man, the one who would do anything to protect me? Or was he someone else, someone who would protect himself first? He had to know I'd find out at some point, and then what? Then what for me? Would he have told me had he not died? I sat at the kitch-en table and let the news circulate through my arteries and veins, throbbing into every organ, every cell.

"Did he go see her?"

My mother didn't know.

"You didn't ask?"

She shook her head.

"And when he died, you didn't tell us. And before that, when we grew up?"

"What for?"

"What for? She's a human being, a sister, a not-dead, living sister. Of mine. Maybe she'd want to know Ben and me. Maybe we'd want to know her. These are people, for god's sake."

"It happened before you."

"That is psychotic. It's happening now. Maybe not anymore for you, but for me. I had a right to know."

"It was his tale to tell."

I stood quickly from the chair and felt faint, steadying myself on the table before leaving the room. I never considered this sort of situation. In thinking about my father's affect that day, that desperation, I had thought that maybe he had done something he shouldn't have, crossed a line of some kind to help a patient or a friend. And that my knowing would be bad for me, would somehow implicate me. I believed that his silence was protection, mine, not his. As the years went on, I thought that whatever it was that had tormented him would have had a shelf life and been long gone. Its significance, and effect, would have evaporated with time. But this secret grew worse, with each second it was concealed.

At the doorway, I turned back. "What is her name?"

My mother hesitated. "Anna."

I stared.

"Fitzpatrick. Mother's name is Claire."

"Where?"

"Attleboro."

THIRTY-EIGHT

FOLLOWING HER ACCIDENT, JEFF agreed that it was best for Roxy to sleep at home until she felt comfortable staying overnight, at whatever age that might be. She was always happy to see him, and the crying stopped when he picked her up. It was the right decision for everyone, and I was relieved that Jeff didn't make it difficult.

My mother went home to New York at the end of that week, and it took a bit for life to normalize. Roxy went back to school with a walking boot on her foot, and I returned to the office. Carolina Cupcakes was evicted and sued for back rent, and detectives caught up with the culprits, who had fled to Georgia. When my story was published, former customers brought a class action suit, claiming fraud. They rallied in front of the shop, chanting, "Faker Bakers, Pay Us Back!"

Several weeks later, Papa Sam's dress arrived in the mail. Pale blue and lavender organza rippled from the tissue, filling with air. Muted with age, they were Renoir shades, happy, yet sophisticated. The gown still had some of the stiffness that new fabric has—perhaps it hadn't seen many parties—and I noticed a spray of bugle beads that I hadn't seen in the picture. I hung the dress on a velvet hanger in Roxy's closet and ran my fingers over the label. Lill-Dor Fashions Inc. Art nouveau lettering in claret. Tears in my eyes.

When Roxy saw it, she gasped. I took it down and held it up to her. "Can I wear it when I'm bigger? When I'm seven?"

"Whenever it fits. It's yours. My grandpa made it, and he made one just like it for me when I was younger."

She smoothed out the skirt with her tiny hands. "We can be twins."

"Is this Claire Fitzpatrick?" I said into the phone.

The voice on the other end was cheery and strong. When I worked for the college radio station, I learned to smile as I delivered the news. It made the sound of the words engaging and friendly. Claire Fitzpatrick knew the trick.

There was no way to ease into a conversation. I couldn't remind her of her dalliance with my father in the late 1950s, or the resulting child who was now an adult, or the concealment of her existence all of these decades. I could only be direct. My name would be enough.

"This is Kate Nichols, Richard Nichols' daughter." I waited. "Claire?"

"Give me a minute, dear." A few seconds went by. "I suppose I've been waiting for this call."

"I'm sorry for contacting you out of the blue." I didn't know if she'd be resentful or appreciative or stunned or angry. Or all of those things.

"Please don't apologize. I'm happy that you called." I heard her inhale. "I guess you want to know about Anna."

"I do, if that's okay with you. I just found out about her."

"Just?"

"A long time, I know..."

"Then you must have questions."

"So many." I looked at my notes. "Did she know him, or know of him?"

Claire hesitated. "I think that Anna can tell you better."

"Would she talk to me?"

"She's been waiting to talk to you. I'll give her your number."

The next day, Anna and I spoke on the phone. I learned that for eighteen years, my father drove one hundred and fifty-two miles once a month to meet her and her mother for lunch at a diner in Warwick, Rhode Island, twenty miles south of their home in Attleboro, Massachusetts. Two hundred and sixteen times, he got into his Bonneville, and later the Oldsmobile that we took to Belle Harbor, and he didn't go to the hospital and remove bowel obstructions and eat the Salisbury Steak from the cafeteria. He didn't walk in wearing his sports coat and striped tie and change into the scrubs, with the surgeon's cap and surgeon's shoe covers, and sterilize each of his hands, front and back, back and front, for a full five minutes, brushing under each nail, around each wrist and forearm, up to the elbow. He didn't cut into flesh and save the organ or the life and then close up, sewing with beautiful, even stitches that wouldn't dare pucker or pull, that would fade with time or exist in shadow, a hint of what was, what is now better. No, he drove to Warwick, Rhode Island, to repair this other mishap, or try to, knowing that another wound would emerge, needing fixing, if not then, at some point.

It was to be me, the child who chose words instead of scalpels, who would operate, who would diagnose and treat, who would hope for an optimal result. Who would do no harm.

My father ordered the turkey club, always. Extra pickles. They sat in a booth. Anna knew him as her father. He wasn't ever a "friend of the family" or an "uncle." They talked about school, her friends, cello. She played the cello. There was no calling in between visits. He never met her siblings or attended a concert or birthday party. He had lunch. The turkey club. And that was it. She loved him just the same. It was enough. It was all that she knew.

When she was old enough to realize that he could have other children, she asked to meet them, and he said that one day, she could. Her mother explained what had happened when she was fifteen.

"It was a secret in your family, so it wasn't up to me," she said. I heard a catch in her throat. "I had to wait for you."

She waited forty-eight years.

THIRTY-NINE

ON A SATURDAY MORNING six months later, I woke up at six-thirty and put on a dress. A print of wispy rosebuds and forget-me-knots, pinks and blues. I pulled my hair to the side in a barrette and clasped Grandma Lilly's locket behind my neck.

"You look nice," said Jeff when I opened the door. "Ready?"

"I am, thanks. She's still sleeping, but she knows you'll be here when she gets up. Lunch and dinner are in the fridge, and she said she wanted to go to the Shady Park. Bug spray is by the washing machine."

"Got it."

"Oh, and she's liking avocados lately."

"Don't worry, we'll have a good time."

"I'll be back by seven. At the latest." I tied a sweater around my waist and stashed a trowel in my handbag, wrapped in plastic.

Jeff started to ask.

"I'm doing something with it."

"I hope so."

"Coffee's made." I closed the door behind me and opened it again. "You have to turn off the pot. It's not automatic."

"Turn off the pot, check. Really. Go, or you'll miss your flight."

I flew to LaGuardia, rented a car and drove fourteen miles to Elmont, New York. Along the way, I stopped at a nursery I had tracked down earlier in the week and bought a pot of hydrangeas.

The entrance to Acadia Cemetery was marked with two stone columns and boxwood hedges, cut into symmetrical slopes. I turned into the driveway and followed the signs to the office.

Inside, a man worked behind a desk. He looked up when I entered. "Would you like a map?"

I nodded. "And I'd like to arrange for a plot to be cared for." I took out a pad on which I had written the details. Section F, Block 3, Row D, Grave 4. "I called some months ago and was told it hadn't been mowed or anything."

He checked his files. "Nope, never. Hmm, long time. It will be $150 per year."

"And a stone. A footstone. Can I order one here?"

"Mmm-hmm."

I opened up my pad and put it on the counter. "This is what I want it to say."

Abraham Goldman, 1932. Born from love. Cherished, still.

He looked over his glasses. "Only one year?"

"Four days."

The man tilted his head. "It's a nice inscription." He gave me a map.

I got back into the car and followed the route to Section F, Block 3. From there, I walked to the row, gravel crunching under my feet, the hydrangea plant heavy in my hand. I turned and counted to the fourth grave, passing a row of headstones. The Bravermans. I stopped in front of the patch of land, overgrown, but not as messy as I'd expected. To its right, there was another marker, just one, Marie Greenstein. Good company, I thought.

Here I stood, at the place where he was, where fear and sorrow and mystery convened, a maelstrom above his tiny form, separate from him, unknown to him. It had hovered for eight decades, here, and in different ways in all of us. I didn't know where to step, what to touch. I trembled at the edge, beneath the churn, the unrest. Determining where he may have laid, I walked onto the grass below him, setting down the hydrangeas and trowel and lowering myself to my knees. I pulled the weeds and smoothed the grass, something in me feeling the swirl quiet and slow and fall away.

I picked up the trowel and pressed its point into the earth. A circle emerged and then a hole. I tipped the pot and pulled out the plant, gripping it below the blooms, glorious shades of blue, the aquamarines and cornflowers and teals. With two palms, I lowered it into the dirt and sat back on my heels. Grandma Lilly's locket swung and tapped my chest. I settled it down and held on for a moment, closing my eyes in the northeastern sun. My grandparents were present, in the pendant in my hand, with their infant son. I unlatched the clasp behind my neck and opened the locket, their faces revealed one last time. They flickered and twirled in the New York sky, descending like fairy dust into the soil.

AUTHOR'S NOTE

THE BABY WHO IS portrayed in this book would have been my uncle. The circumstances surrounding his death were not revealed to his parents–my grandparents–and remained a mystery for decades. While most of the book's details about his and his parents' life are true, certain names, places, characters and incidents are products of my imagination.

Made in United States
North Haven, CT
02 June 2023

37271626R00131